Dear Reader

When two brothers love the same woman, the result is a mighty clash in the fierce heat of Tuscany, a place where the air crackles with danger.

Rinaldo and Gino share a powerful love of the land, and have the same emotional, virile intensity. But fate has turned Rinaldo into a gruff, hard-bitten cynic, while Gino, his younger brother, likes to laugh, and still has traces of the boy in his carefree nature.

Their peace is wrecked by Alex, from England, who has unexpectedly inherited a claim to some of their farm. Then no amount of brotherly love can count against the passion for a woman both see as an interloper, yet whom neither can resist.

Elegant, determined, a success in her high-powered career, Alex is sure she can deal with the Farnese brothers. She doesn't know that they have tossed a coin for her, nor would she care. She will choose the man she wants.

One will win the prize. The other will be cast out to find his destiny among strangers.

Lucy Gordon

Lucy Gordon cut her writing teeth on magazine journalism, interviewing many of the world's most interesting men, including Warren Beatty, Richard Chamberlain, Roger Moore, Sir Alec Guinness and Sir John Gielgud. She also camped out with lions in Africa, and had many other unusual experiences which have often provided the background for her books. She is married to a Venetian, whom she met while on holiday in Venice. They got engaged within two days. Two of her books have won the Romance Writers of America RITA® award, SONG OF THE LORELEI in 1990, and HIS BROTHER'S CHILD in 1998 in the Best Traditional Romance category. You can visit her website at www.zyworld.com/LucyGordon

Recent titles by the same author:

THE ITALIAN'S BABY
THE VENETIAN PLAYBOY'S BRIDE*
THE ITALIAN MILLIONAIRE'S MARRIAGE*
THE TUSCAN TYCOON'S WIFE*

The Counts of Calvani trilogy

RINALDO'S INHERITED BRIDE

BY

LUCY GORDON

MILLS & BOON®

MILLS & BOON and MILLS & BOON with the Rose Device are registered trademarks of the publisher.

First published in Great Britain 2004
Harlequin Mills & Boon Limited,
Eton House, 18-24 Paradise Road, Richmond, Surrey TW9 1SR

© Lucy Gordon 2004

ISBN 0 263 83829 3

Set in Times Roman 10½ on 12 pt.
02-0604-47966

Printed and bound in Spain
by Litografía Rosés, S.A., Barcelona

CHAPTER ONE

'HE HATES me. He really hates me!'

Alex had expected some resentment, but not this bleak hostility. All the way out from England to Italy she had wondered about Rinaldo and Gino Farnese, the two men she had partly dispossessed.

Now, meeting Rinaldo's eyes across his father's grave, she thought she had never seen so much concentrated bitterness in one human being.

She blinked, thinking it might be an illusion of the brilliant Italian sun. Here there were sharp edges like sword blades, and dark shadows that swallowed light; hot colours, red, orange, deep yellow, black. Vibrant. Intense. Dangerous.

Now I'm getting fanciful, she thought.

But the danger was there, in the fury-filled eyes of Rinaldo Farnese, still watching her.

Isidoro, her elderly Italian lawyer, had pointed out the two Farnese brothers, but even without that she would have known them. The family likeness was clear. Both men were tall, with lean, fine-featured faces and dark, brilliant eyes.

Gino, clearly the younger, looked as though he had a softer side. There was a touch of curl in his hair, and a curve to his mouth that suggested humour, flirtation, delight.

But there was nothing soft about Rinaldo. His face might have been carved from granite. He seemed to be in his late thirties, with a high forehead and a nose that only just escaped being hooked. It was the most powerful feature in a powerful face.

Even at this distance Alex could detect a tension so fierce that it threatened to tear him apart. He was holding it back with a supreme effort. His grim, taut mouth revealed that, and the set of his chin.

There would be no yielding from him, Alex thought. No relenting. No forgiveness.

But why should she think she needed forgiveness from Rinaldo Farnese? She'd done him no wrong.

But he had been wronged, not by her, but by the father who had mortgaged a third of the family property, and left his sons to find out, brutally, after his death.

'Vincente Farnese was a delightful fellow,' Isidoro had told her. 'But he had this terrible habit of putting off awkward moments and hoping for a miracle. Rinaldo took charge as much as possible, but the old boy still left him a nasty surprise at the end. Can't blame him for being a bit put out.'

But the man facing her over the grave wasn't 'a bit put out.' He was ready to do murder.

'I guess I shouldn't have come to their father's funeral,' she murmured to Isidoro.

'No, they probably think you're gloating.'

'I just wanted to meet them, reassure them that I'll give them a fair chance to redeem the mortgage.'

'Alex, haven't you understood? As far as these men are concerned they owe you nothing, and you're a usurper. Offering a ''fair chance'' to pay you is a recipe for bloodshed. Let's get out of here fast.'

'You go. I'm not running away from them.'

'You may wish you had,' he said gloomily.

'Nonsense, what can they do to me?'

It had seemed so easy a week ago, sitting in the elegant London restaurant with David.

'This inheritance will probably pay for your partnership,' he'd observed.

'And a lot of other things too,' she said, smiling, and thinking of the dream home that they would share after their wedding.

David didn't answer this directly, but he raised his champagne glass in salute.

David Edwards was part of Alex's life plan. At forty, neatly handsome in a pin-striped kind of way, he was the head of a firm of very expensive, very prestigious London accountants.

Alex had started work for them eight years ago, after passing her accountancy exams with top honours. She had always known that one day she would be a partner, just as one day she would marry David.

Eight years had transformed her from a rather shy, awkward girl, more at home with figures than people, into a stunning, sophisticated woman.

It was David himself who had unknowingly started the transformation in her early days with the firm. Struck by his looks, she had longed to attract his attention.

After six months, without success, she had overheard him casually asking a colleague, 'Who's the pudding in the red dress?'

He had passed on, unaware that the 'pudding' had heard him and was choking back misery and anger.

Two days later David announced his engagement to the daughter of the senior partner.

Alex had plunged into her work. For the next five years she allowed herself only the most passing relationships. At the end of that time her long hours and excellent results had made her a power in the firm.

By then the senior partner had retired and David had taken over the position. Now he no longer needed his father-in-law's influence, although it was only ill-natured people who openly made a connection between that and his divorce.

Alex had worked as hard on transforming herself as she had on her job. Her body represented the triumph of the workout. Her legs were long and slender enough to risk the shortest skirts. The tightest of dresses found no extra pounds on her.

Her fair hair was short, expertly cut and shaped, nestling close to her neat head on top of a long, elegant neck. She was a highly finished work of art, her mind as perfectly ordered as her appearance.

She and David became an item, and everyone knew that soon the firm's two stars would link up and run the place together.

Now it seemed that nothing could be better structured. Her inheritance would be followed by her partnership, and then by her marriage.

'Of course it might take a little time to arrange,' David mused now. 'You haven't actually inherited part of the property, have you?'

'No, just the money that was loaned against it. Enrico assigned the debt to me in his will. So the Farnese brothers owe me a large sum of money, and if they can't repay in a reasonable time, that's when I can claim some of the actual farm.'

'Either that or sell your interest to someone else, which would make more sense. What would you want with one third of a farm?'

'Nothing, but I'd feel uneasy about doing that. I have to give the Farneses every chance to pay me first.'

'Sure, and, as I said, it may take time. So don't rush back. Take as long as you need and do it properly.'

Alex smiled, thinking fondly how understanding he was. It would make everything easier.

'You haven't seen much of your Italian relatives, have you?' David asked now.

'My mother was Enrico Mori's niece. He came to visit us a couple of times. He was an excitable man, very intense and emotional. Just like her.'

'But not like you?'

She laughed. 'Well, I couldn't afford to be intense and emotional. Mum filled the house with her melodrama. I adored her, but I suppose I developed my common sense as a reaction. One of us had to be cool, calm and collected.

'I remember Enrico frowning and saying, "You must be like your English Poppa," and it wasn't a compliment. Poppa died when I was twelve, but I remember he never shouted or lost his temper.'

'And you don't either.'

'What's the point? It's better to talk things out sensibly. Mum used to say that one day we'd visit Italy together, and I'd "see the light". She even raised me to speak Italian and some Tuscan dialect, so that I wouldn't be all at sea when we visited "my other country".'

'But you never went?'

'She became ill. When she died three years ago Enrico came over and I met him again.'

'Are you his only heir?'

'No, there are some distant cousins who inherit his house and land. He was a rich man, with no wife or children. He lived alone in Florence, having a great old time, drinking and chasing women.'

'So where did Vincente Farnese come into this?'

'They were old friends. A few years ago he borrowed some money from Enrico, and charged it against Belluna, that's the farm. Last week, apparently, they went out on a binge, drove the car home, and had the accident that killed them both.'

'And his sons had no idea that there was a hefty mortgage against the land?'

'Not until Enrico's will was read, apparently.'

'So you're going right into the lion's den? Be careful.'

'You surely don't think I'll be assassinated down a dark lane? I shall go to Florence, make an arrangement with the Farnese brothers, and then come home.'

'And if they can't raise the money, and you sell your interest to an outsider? Will they sit quiet for that?'

'Don't be melodramatic, David,' she said, laughing. 'I'm sure they're reasonable people, just as I am. We'll sort it all out, somehow.'

'Reasonable?' Rinaldo snapped. 'Our father charged a huge loan against this property without telling us, and the lawyers want us to be reasonable?'

Gino sighed. 'I still can't take it in,' he said. 'How could Poppa have kept such a secret for so long, especially from you?'

The light was fading, for the evening was well advanced. Standing by the window of his home, looking out over the hills and fields that stretched into the distance, earth that he had cultivated with his own hands, sometimes at terrible cost, Rinaldo knew that he must cling onto this, or go mad.

'You and I are Poppa's heirs and the legal owners of Belluna,' Gino pointed out. 'This woman can't change that.'

'She can if we can't pay up. If she doesn't get her cash

she can claim one third of Belluna. Poppa never made
any repayments, so now we owe the whole amount, plus
interest.'

'Well, I suppose we gained from having all that
money,' Gino mused.

'That's true,' Rinaldo admitted reluctantly. 'It paid for
the new machinery, the hire of extra labourers, the best
fertiliser, which has greatly improved our crops. All that
cost a fortune. Poppa just said he'd won the lottery.'

'And we believed it until the wills were read,' Gino
said heavily. 'That's what hurts, that he left us to find
out like that.' But then he gave a heavy sigh. 'Still, I
suppose we shouldn't blame him. He didn't know he was
going to die suddenly. Do we know anything about this
woman, apart from the fact that she's English?'

'According to the lawyer her name is Alexandra Dacre.
She's in her late twenties, an accountant, and lives in
London.'

'I don't like the sound of her,' Gino sighed.

'Neither do I. This is a cold-blooded Anglo-Saxon. She
works with money, and that's all she'll care about.'

He raised his head suddenly, and there was a fierce
intensity in his eyes.

'We have no choice,' he said. *'We have to get rid of
her.'*

Gino jumped. *'How? Rinaldo, for pity's sake—!'*

At that moment he could have believed his brother
capable of any cruel act.

Rinaldo gave a brief smile, which had the strange effect of making his face even more grim than before.

'Calm down,' he said. 'I'm not planning murder. I
don't say the idea isn't appealing, but it's not what I
meant. I want to dispose of her legally.'

'So we have to pay her.'

'How? All the money we have is ploughed into the land until harvest. We're already overdrawn at the bank, and a loan would be at a ruinous rate of interest.'

'Can't our lawyer suggest something?'

'He's going soft in the head. Since she's single he had the brilliant idea that one of us marry her.'

'That's it!' Gino cried. 'The perfect answer. All problems solved.'

He spread his hands in a triumphant gesture and gave his attractive, easy laugh. He was twenty-seven and there was still a touch of the boy about him.

'So now we have to meet her,' he said. 'I wonder if she'll come to Poppa's funeral?'

'She won't dare!' Rinaldo snapped. 'Now, come and have supper. Teresa's been getting it ready.'

In the kitchen they found Teresa, the elderly housekeeper, laying the table. As she worked she wept. It had been like that every day since Vincente had died.

Rinaldo wasn't hungry, but he knew that to say so would be to upset the old woman even more. Instead he placed a gentle hand on her shoulder, silently comforting her until she stopped weeping.

'That's better now,' he said kindly. 'You know how Poppa hated long faces.'

She nodded. 'Always laughing,' she said huskily. 'Even if the crops failed, he would find something to laugh at. He was a rare one.'

'Yes, he was,' Rinaldo agreed. 'And we must remember him like that.'

She looked at the chair by the great kitchen range, where Vincente had often sat.

'He should be there,' she said. 'Telling funny stories, making silly jokes. Do you remember how terrible his jokes were?'

Rinaldo nodded. 'And the worst puns I ever heard.'

Gino came in and gave Teresa a big, generous hug. He was a young man who hugged people easily, and it made him loved wherever he went. Now it was enough to start her crying again, and he held her patiently in his strong arms until she was ready to stop.

Rinaldo left them and went outside. When he'd gone Teresa muttered, 'He's lost so many of those he loved, and each time I've seen his face grow a little darker, a little more bleak.'

Gino nodded. He knew Teresa was talking about Rinaldo's wife Maria, and their baby son, both dead in the second year of their marriage.

'If they'd lived, the little boy would have been nearly ten by now,' he reflected. 'And they'd probably have had several more children. This house would have been full of kids. I'd have had nephews and nieces to teach mischief to, instead of—'

He looked up at the building that was much too large for the three people who shared it.

'Now he only has you,' Teresa agreed.

'And you. And that daft mutt. Sometimes I think Brutus means more to him than any other creature, because he was Maria's dog. Apart from that he loves the farm, and he's possessive about it because he has so little else. I hope Signorina Dacre has a lot of nerve, because she's going to need it.'

Rinaldo returned with the large indeterminate animal Gino had stigmatised as 'that daft mutt'. Brutus had an air of amiability mixed with anarchy, plus huge feet. Ignoring Teresa's look of disapproval he parked himself under the table, close to his master.

Over pasta and mushrooms Gino said, lightly, 'So I suppose one of us has to marry the English woman.'

'When you say "one of us" you mean me, I suppose,' Rinaldo growled. 'You wouldn't like settling down with a wife, not if it meant having to stop your nonsense. Besides, she evidently has an orderly mind, which means she'd be driven nuts by you in five minutes.'

'Then you should be the one,' Gino said.

'No, thank you.' Rinaldo's tone was a warning.

'But you're the head of the family now. I think it's your duty. Hey—what are you doing with that wine?'

'Preparing to pour it over your head if you don't shut up.'

'But we have to do something. We need a master plan.'

His brother replaced the wine on the table, annoyance giving way to faint amusement. Gino's flippancy might often be annoying, but it was served up with a generous helping of charm.

Rinaldo would have declared himself immune to that charm. Even so, he regarded his brother with a wry look that was almost a grin.

'Then get to work,' he said. 'Make her head spin.'

'I've got a better idea. Let's toss for her.'

'For pity's sake grow up!'

'Seriously, let Fate make the decision.'

'If I go through with this charade, I don't want to hear it mentioned again. Hurry up and get it over with!'

Gino took a coin from his pocket and flipped it high in the air. 'Call!'

'Tails.'

Gino caught the coin and slapped it down on the back of his hand.

'Tails!' he said. 'She's all yours.'

Rinaldo groaned. 'I thought you were using your two-headed coin or I wouldn't have played.'

'As if I'd do a thing like that!' Gino sounded aggrieved.

'I've known times when—well, never mind. I'm not interested. You can have her.'

He rose and drained his glass before Gino could answer. He didn't feel that he could stand much more of this conversation.

Gino went to bed first. He was young. Even in his grief for a beloved father he slept easily.

Rinaldo could barely remember what it was to sleep peacefully. When the house was quiet he slipped out. The moon was up, casting a livid white glow over the earth. The light was neither soft nor alluring, but harsh, showing him outlines of trees and hills in brutal relief.

That was the land to which he'd given his whole life. Here, in this soft earth, he'd lain one night with a girl who smelled of flowers and joy, whispering words of love.

'Soon it will be our wedding day, love of my life—come to me—be mine always.'

And she had come to him in passion and tenderness, generous and giving, nothing held back, her body young and pliable in his arms.

But for such a little time.

One year and six months from the date of their wedding to the day he'd buried his wife and child together.

And his heart with them.

He walked on. He could have trodden this journey with his eyes closed. Every inch of this land was part of his being. He knew its moods, how it could be harsh, brutal, sometimes generous with its bounty but more often demanding a cruel price.

Until today he had paid the price, not always willingly, sometimes in anguish and bitterness, but he had paid it.

And now this.

He lost track of time, seeing nothing with his outer eye. What he could see, inwardly, was Vincente, roaring with laughter as he tossed his baby son, Gino, up into the air, then turned to smile lovingly on the child Rinaldo.

'Remember when I used to do that with you, my son? Now we are men together.'

And his own eager response. 'Yes, Poppa!'

He had been eight years old, and his father had known by instinct what to say to drive out jealousy of the new baby, and make him happy.

Poppa, who had believed that the world was a good place because there was always warmth and love and generosity, and who had tried to make him believe it too.

Poppa, his ally in a hundred childhood pranks. 'We won't tell Mamma, it would only worry her.'

But these images were succeeded by another, one he hadn't seen, but which he now realised had been there all along: the old man, round faced and white whiskered, laughing up his sleeve at the little joke he'd played on his sons, and particularly on his forceful elder son.

Vincente hadn't seen the danger. So there had been no warning, no chance to be prepared. Rinaldo had always loved his father, but at this moment it was hard not to hate him.

The darkness was turning to the first grey of dawn. He had walked for miles, and now it was time to walk back and make ready for the biggest fight of his life.

CHAPTER TWO

RINALDO FARNESE finally dragged his eyes away from
the woman who was his enemy. He had noted dispas-
sionately that she was beautiful in a glossy, city-bred kind
of way that would have increased his hostility if it hadn't
been at fever pitch already. Everything about her confirmed his suspicions, from her fair hair to her elegant
clothes.

It was time for the mourners to speak over the grave.
There were many, for Vincente had been popular. Some
were elderly men, 'partners in crime' who had spent days
in the sun with him, drinking wine and remembering the
old times.

There were several middle-aged and elderly women,
hinting wistfully at sweet memories, under the jealous
eyes of their menfolk.

Finally there were his sons. Gino spoke movingly, re-
calling his father's gentleness and sweet temper, his ready
laughter.

'He'd had a hard life,' he recalled, 'working very long
hours, every day for years, so that his family might prosper. But it never soured him, and to the end of his life,
nothing delighted him as much as a practical joke.'

Then he fell silent, and a soft ripple ran around the
crowd. By now all of them knew about Vincente's last
practical joke.

A heaviness seemed to come over Gino as he realised
what he had said. The light went out of his attractive

young face, and his eyes sought his brother with a touch of desperation.

Rinaldo's face revealed nothing. With a brief nod at Gino he stepped up to take his place.

'My father was a man who could win love,' he said, speaking almost curtly. 'That much is proved by the presence of so many of his friends today. It is no more than he deserved. I thank each of you for coming to do him honour.'

That was all. The words were jerked from him as if by force. His face might have been made of stone.

The mourners began to drift away from the grave. Rinaldo gave Alex a last look and turned, touching Gino's arm to indicate for him to come too.

'Wait,' Gino said.

'No,' Rinaldo was following his gaze.

'We've got to meet her some time. Besides—' he gave a soft whistle. 'She's beautiful.'

'Remember where you are and show respect,' Rinaldo said quietly.

'Poppa wouldn't mind. He'd have been the first to whistle. Rinaldo, have you ever seen such a beauty?'

'I'm happy for you,' his brother said without looking at him. 'Your job should be easier.'

Gino had caught the lawyer's eye and raised his eyebrows, inclining his head slightly in Alex's direction. Isidoro nodded and Gino began to make his way across to them.

Alex caught the look they exchanged, then she focused on Gino. An engaging young man, she thought. Even dressed in black, he had a kind of brightness about him. His handsome face was fresh, eager, open.

It had little to do with his youth. It was more a natural

joyousness in his nature that would be with him all his life, unless something happened to sour it.

'Gino, this is Signorina Alexandra Dacre,' Isidoro hastened to make the introductions. 'Enrico was her great-uncle.'

'Yes, I've heard of Signorina Dacre.' Gino's smile had an almost conspiratorial quality, as if to suggest that they were all in this mess together.

'I'm beginning to feel as if the whole of Florence has heard of me,' she said, smiling back and beginning to like him.

'The whole of Tuscany,' he said. 'Sensations like this don't happen every day.'

'I gather you knew nothing about it,' Alex said.

'Nothing at all, until the lawyers were going through the paperwork.'

'What a nasty shock. I'm surprised you want to shake my hand.'

'It isn't your fault,' Gino said at once.

His grasp, like everything about him, was warm, enclosing her hand in both of his.

'We must meet properly and talk,' he said.

'Yes, there's a lot to talk about,' she agreed. Suddenly she burst out, 'Did I do wrong to come to your father's funeral? Perhaps it was tasteless of me, but I only—look, I meant well.'

'Yes, it was tasteless of you,' said a dry, ironic voice. 'You have no place here. Why did you come?'

'Rinaldo, please,' Gino said in a swift, soft voice.

'No, he's right,' Alex said hastily. 'I made a mistake. I'll go now.'

'But we're having a reception in the Hotel Favello,' Gino said. 'Enrico was Poppa's dearest friend, and you're part of Enrico's family, so naturally you're invited.'

He glanced at his brother, waiting for his confirmation. For a moment Rinaldo's manners warred with his hostility. At last he shrugged and said briefly, 'Of course.'

He turned away without waiting for her answer.

'The hotel isn't far,' Gino said. 'I'll show you.'

'No need, I'm staying there,' Alex told him. 'I arrived last night.'

'Then shall we go?' He offered her his arm.

'Thank you, but I'll make my own way. You have guests who'll want your attention.'

She hurried away before he could argue, and rejoined Isidoro, who fell into step beside her.

'If you're going into the lion's den I'm coming with you,' he said.

'That might be a good idea after all,' she agreed.

As they walked the short distance to the hotel Alex said, 'He really did have a lot of friends, didn't he?'

'Yes, he was a much-loved man. But the people at the wake won't just be his friends and lovers. They'll be the vultures hovering over that mortgage, and you'll be very interesting to them.

'Watch out for a man called Montelli. He's greedy and unscrupulous, and if Rinaldo sees you talking to him it'll make him mad.'

'Well,' Alex said, apparently considering this, 'since everything I do is going to make that man angry, I think I'll just go right ahead and do what suits me.'

The Hotel Favello was a Renaissance building that had once belonged to the Favello family, wealthy and influential for centuries, now fallen on hard times.

It had been turned into a luxury hotel in such a way that every modern comfort was provided, but so discreetly that nothing seemed to have changed for centuries.

Alex went up to her room first, so as not to arrive too soon, wishing she had time for a shower. It was June and Florence was hotter than anything she had experienced in England. Standing in the sun, she had felt the heat spreading over her skin beneath her clothes, making her intensely aware of every inch of her body.

But there was no time for a shower if she were to join the reception. She mopped her brow and checked her appearance in the mirror. She looked, as always, immaculate.

It would have been over-the-top to wear black for a man she hadn't known, but she was formally dressed in a navy blue linen dress, with a matching coat, adorned only by one silver brooch. Now she tossed aside the coat before going downstairs.

She was relieved to see that the reception room was already crowded, so that she attracted little attention.

Isidoro scuttled to greet her and pointed out some of the others.

'The ones glowering at you in the corner are the other members of Enrico's family,' he said.

'Don't tell me they're annoyed with me too?' she exclaimed.

'Of course. They were expecting to inherit more.'

'So I'm in the firing line from both sides,' she said with a touch of exasperation. 'Oh, heavens!'

'This is Italy,' Isidoro said wryly. 'The home of the blood feud. Here they come.'

Two men and two women appeared solidly before Alex. Greetings were exchanged, not overtly hostile, but cautious. The older man, who seemed to be the spokesman for the group, muttered something about having 'necessary discussions' later.

Alex nodded agreement, and the group moved off. But

behind them was a middle-aged man of large proportions and an oily manner. He introduced himself as Leo Montelli, and said that the sooner they talked the better.

After him came another local landowner, and after him came the representative of a bank. Alex began to feel dizzy. One thing was clear. The message about who she was and why she was here had gone out loud and clear to everyone in the room.

It had certainly reached Rinaldo Farnese, who was watching her steadily. His face was inscrutable, but Alex had the feeling that he was mentally taking notes.

'Isidoro, I'm leaving,' she said. 'This shouldn't be happening here. It isn't seemly.'

'Shall I fix appointments with them for you?'

'Not yet,' she said quickly. 'I must talk to the Farneses first. For now I'll just slip away.'

'Look,' Isidoro said.

Rinaldo was cutting his way through the crowd until he reached her and said very softly, 'I want you to leave, right now. Your behaviour is unseemly.'

'Hey, now look—'

'How dare you dance on my father's grave! Leave right this moment or I'll put you out myself.'

'*Signore*—' Isidoro was vainly trying to claim his attention.

'I was about to leave anyway,' Alex said.

'To be sure, *signorina*, I believe you.'

'You'd better,' she said losing her temper. 'Signor Farnese, I dislike you at least as much as you dislike me, and I won't stand for being called a liar. If this wasn't a solemn occasion I would take the greatest pleasure in losing my temper in a way you wouldn't forget.'

She stormed out without giving him the chance to answer. If she could have sold the entire farm out from under him she would have done so at that moment.

The Hotel Favello was in the Piazza della Republica, in the medieval heart of Florence. Here Alex was close to the great buildings, the Palazzo Vecchio, the Duomo, whose huge bulk dominated the Florence skyline, the fascinating Ponte Vecchio over the River Arno, and many other places she had promised herself that she would visit before she left.

On the evening of the funeral she decided to eat out, preferably in a restaurant where she could gain a floodlit view of the buildings.

She'd had a shower as soon as she left the reception, but before getting dressed she had another one under cold water. Thankfully the onset of evening was making temperatures fall, and the room had good air-conditioning, but she felt as though the heat had penetrated down to the core of her.

She started to put on a pair of tights, but discarded them almost at once, disliking the suffocating sensation of anything clinging to her flesh. She rejected a bra for the same reason.

When she finally slipped on a white silk dress she wore only a slip and brief panties beneath, because that was the only way she felt her body could breathe.

Just as she was about to leave there was a knock on her door.

She opened it to find Rinaldo Farnese standing there.

He had removed the jacket of his smart black suit, and was holding it hooked over the shoulder of his white shirt, which had been pulled open at the throat. His hair was untidy, his face weary, and he looked as though he had discarded the strait-laced persona of the funeral with as much relief as she had discarded her coat.

'This won't take long,' he said, pushing the door further open and walking into the room.

'Hey, I didn't invite you in,' she protested.

'I didn't invite you either, but here you are,' he responded.

'And I'm just going out to dinner,' she said.

At this point a gentleman would have at least offered her a drink. Rinaldo's only response was a shrug.

'Then I'll be brief,' he said.

'Please do,' she replied crisply.

'First, I suppose I owe you an apology for my behaviour this afternoon.'

She gaped at him, totally taken aback. The last thing she had expected from this man was an apology.

'After you left I spoke to Isidoro who confirmed that you'd been about to depart of your own accord, and that you too had used the word unseemly.' He took a deep breath and spoke as though the words were jerked from him. 'I apologise for doubting your truthfulness.'

'I appreciate that,' she said, 'all the more because it half killed you to say it.'

'I'm not known for my social skills,' he agreed wryly.

'I'd never have guessed.'

'You think to disconcert me with irony? Don't bother.' She nodded.

'You're right. You don't care enough about other people's opinions to mind whether you have social skills or not,' she said gravely. 'I'm sure rudeness has its advantages, besides being less trouble.'

This time there was no doubt that she got to him. He eyed her narrowly. Alex looked straight back at him.

'May I remind you that I only came to that reception

on your brother's invitation?' she said. 'It wasn't my idea, and I certainly wouldn't have come if I'd known what would happen. Perhaps it's I who owe you an apology for my clumsiness.'

They regarded each other warily, neither of them in the least mollified by the other's conciliatory words.

Despite her exasperation Alex was curious about him. After the sleek, smooth men she knew in London, meeting Rinaldo was like encountering a wild animal. The feelings that drove him were so powerful that she could almost feel them radiating from him. He was controlling them, but only just.

She thought of David, who never did anything that hadn't been planned beforehand. She couldn't imagine him losing control, but with Rinaldo Farnese she could imagine it only too easily.

Strangely the thought did not alarm her, but only increased her curiosity.

He began to stride impatiently about the room in a way that told her he was happier outdoors, and rooms suffocated him. Now she appreciated how tall he was, over six foot, broad-shouldered but lean. He was lithe, not graceful like his brother, but athletic, like a tightly coiled spring.

'So now you've seen them all,' he said. 'All the vultures who are lining up to swoop. They've calculated that your only interest is money. Are they wrong?'

'I—well, you're certainly direct.'

'I came here to know what your plans are. Is that direct enough for you?'

'My plans are fluid at the moment. I'm waiting to see what develops.'

'Do you fancy yourself as a farmer?'

'No, I'm not a farmer, nor do I have any ambitions to be one.'

'That is a wise decision. You would find us two to one against you.'

She surveyed him with her head a little on one side. 'You don't believe in sugar coating it, do you?'

'No,' he said simply, 'there's no point. What are your plans?'

'To discuss the situation with you. The vultures can think what they like. You get the first chance to redeem the loan. Look, I'm not a monster. I know money can be difficult. In my own country I'm an accountant—'

'I know,' he said impatiently. 'Somebody who works with money. And that's all you care about—money.'

'Enough!' she said in a sudden hard voice. 'I won't let you speak to me like that, I'm not responsible for this situation.'

'But you don't mind benefiting from it?'

'I don't mind benefiting under Enrico's will because that's what he wanted. I dare say he would have left me money, but his cash was tied up in you. You're acting as though I have no right to recover it. I'm sorry if it's come as a shock to you, but it isn't my fault that your father didn't tell you.'

'Be silent!' The words were swift and hostile and the look he turned on her was like a dagger. 'Do not speak of my father.'

'All right, but don't blame me for a situation I didn't create.'

He was silent for a moment and she could see that she had taken him aback. After a while he said, 'Nobody doubts your right to accept your inheritance, but I suggest that you be careful how you go about it.'

'What you mean is that you *demand* that I go about it in the way that suits you,' she replied at once.

Something that might almost have been a smile passed over his bleak face and was gone.

'Let us say that you should consider the whole complex situation before you rush to a decision,' he said at last. 'Every penny the farm has is tied up until the harvest. You'll get your money, but in instalments.'

'That's no use to me. I have my own plans.'

He regarded her. 'If your plans conflict with mine, let me advise you to drop them. In the meantime, you should leave Italy.'

'No,' she said bluntly.

'I strongly advise you—'

'The answer is no.'

'*Signorina*,' Rinaldo said softly, 'you do not know this country.'

'All the more reason for remaining. I'm part Italian and this is my country too.'

'You misunderstand. When I said "this country" I didn't mean Italy. I meant Tuscany. You're not in cool, civilised England now. This is a dangerous place for intruders. Those dark hills look inviting, but too often they've hidden brigands who recognised no law but their own.'

'And I'll bet they were led by someone just like you,' she challenged him back. 'Someone who thought he had only to speak and the world trembled. Do you see me trembling?'

'Perhaps you would be wiser if you did.'

'Stop trying to scare me. It won't work. I'll do what suits me, *when* it suits me. If you don't like it—tough. After all, that's the code you live by yourself.'

This was a shot in the dark. She barely knew him, but

instinct would have told her the sort of man he was, even
if his own words and attitude hadn't made it pretty plain.
He was overbearing, and he wouldn't be too scrupulous
about how he got his own way. That was her estimation
of him.

The sooner he realised that, in her, he'd met his match,
the better.

'Are you suggesting that I'm a brigand, *signorina*?'

'I think you could be if you felt it necessary.'

'And *will* it be necessary?'

'You tell me. I imagine we judge the matter differently. I don't want instalments. I need a lump sum, fairly
soon. I have a once-in-a-lifetime chance, and to seize it
I need money. But we can work it out. Perhaps someone
else can take over the mortgage—a bank or something.'

Suddenly his face was dark, distorted.

'Don't try to involve strangers in this,' he said fiercely.
'Do you think I'd allow them to come interfering—dic-
tating—*Maria vergine*!'

He slammed one hand into the other.

'I've had enough of the way you talk to me,' Alex said
firmly. 'Once and for all, try to understand that I will not
be bullied. If you thought I would just collapse, you
picked the wrong person.'

'I'm only trying—'

'I know what you're "only trying" and I've heard
enough. Now I'm going out. If you wish to talk to me
you can make an appointment with my lawyer.'

'The hell I will!'

'The hell you won't!'

Alex snatched up her purse and made for the door.
Grim-faced, he moved fast, and she thought he was going
to bar her way. Instead he opened the door for her and
followed her out.

In the street she walked on without looking where she was going.

'Which of them are you going to meet now?' he demanded, walking beside her.

'Well, of all the—'

'Tell me.'

'It's none of your business.'

He got in front of her, forcing her to stop. 'If you're meeting Montelli it *is* my business.'

'If and when I meet Signor Montelli it will be in my lawyer's office, which is also where I will meet you— always supposing that I *want* to meet you. Now please get out of my way. I'd like to find somewhere to eat.'

Slightly to her surprise he moved aside. 'I can recommend a good place in the next street—'

'You mean it's run by a friend of yours who'll keep an eye on me?' she said lightly.

'You're full of suspicion.'

'Shouldn't I be?'

Wryly, he nodded. 'You're also a very wise woman.'

'Wise enough to pick a restaurant for myself. Your choice might have arsenic in the wine.'

'Only if you have put me in your will.'

The last thing she'd expected from him was a joke, and a choke of laughter burst from her. She controlled it quickly, not wishing to yield a point to him.

Then she turned a corner and stopped in sudden delight at what she saw.

Before her was a huge loggia filled with stalls, selling pictures, ornaments, lace, leather goods, fancy materials. Everywhere was brightly coloured and bustling with life.

Most fascinating of all was a large bronze boar perched on a pedestal which contained a fountain, its tusks gleaming, its mouth open in a grin that mixed ferocity and welcome. Unlike the rest of the body, the nose was gleaming brightly in the late evening sun.

Even as Alex looked, two young women went up to the boar and rubbed its nose.

'That's why it shines,' Rinaldo said. 'You rub the nose and make a wish that one day you'll return to Florence.'

Smiling, Alex put out her hand, but withdrew it without touching the bronze animal.

'I'm not sure what I'll do,' she said, as though considering seriously. 'Wishing to return to Florence would mean that I was leaving, wouldn't it? And that's so much what you're trying to make me do that I think I should do the opposite.'

He eyed her with exasperation. But he did not, as she had been half hoping, show signs of real annoyance.

'Of course, if I just decide to stay here, I wouldn't need to return,' she mused.

'I suppose this entertains you,' he growled. 'To me it's a waste of time.'

'I'm sure you're right. I'll defer a decision until I've worked out what would annoy you the most.'

She began to turn away, but he grasped her upper arm with a hand that could almost encompass it. His grip was light, but she could sense the steel in his fingers, and knew that she had no chance of escape until he released her.

'And then you'll annoy me, for fun,' he said. 'But beware, *signorina*, to me this is not fun. My life's blood is in Belluna. You will remember that, and you will respect it, because if you do not—' his eyes, fixed on hers, were hard as flint '—if you do not—you will wish that you had. I have warned you.'

He removed his hand.

'Enjoy your meal,' he said curtly, and vanished into the crowd.

It was over. He was gone. All the things she ought to have said came crowding into her head now that it was too late to say them. All that was left was the imprint of his hand on the bare skin of her arm. He hadn't held her all that tightly, but she could still feel him.

She turned away from the market and walked on through the streets. She found a restaurant and entered, barely noticing her surroundings.

The food was superb, duck terrine flavoured with black truffle, chick-pea soup with giant prawn tails. She had eaten in the finest restaurants in London and New York, but this was a whole new experience. More art than food.

'Definitely, I am not going home before I have to,' she murmured. 'He can say what he likes.'

CHAPTER THREE

ALEX decided to allow herself the next day for sightseeing. It beat sitting in her room waiting to see what Rinaldo would do next.

But as she descended into the foyer the bulky form of Signor Montelli darkened the door. Alex groaned at the sight of the oily, charmless man whom she remembered from the wake. Reluctantly she sat down with him at a table in the hotel's coffee shop.

'I have come to solve your problems,' he declared loftily.

It was the wrong approach. Alex was immediately antagonised.

'I'm sure that I have no problems that you could possibly know about,' she replied coolly.

'I mean that I'm prepared to pay a high price for your mortgage on the Farnese property. I'm sure we can come to terms.'

'Perhaps we can, but not just yet. I must give the first chance to the Farnese brothers.'

He shrugged dismissively. 'They can't afford it.'

'How do you know how much it is?' she asked curiously.

'Oh—' he said airily, 'these things become known. I'm sure you want to turn your inheritance into cash as soon as possible.'

Since this was precisely why she'd come out to Italy it was unreasonable of Alex to take offence, but she

32

found her resistance stiffening. This man was far too sure
of himself.

'I'm afraid I can't discuss it with you until I've discussed it with them,' she said firmly.

He named a price.

Despite herself Alex was shaken. The money he offered was more than she was owed. The accountant in
her spoke, urging her to close the deal now.

But her sense of justice intervened and made her re-
peat, 'I must speak to them first.'

His eyes narrowed. 'I'm not a patient man, *signorina*.'

'I'll have to take the risk of losing your offer, won't
I?' she said lightly. 'Now, if you'll excuse me.'

As she rose Montelli's hand came out and grasped her
wrist.

'We haven't finished talking.'

'Yes, we have,' she snapped, 'and if you don't release
me right now I shall slap your face so hard that your ears
will be ringing for a week.'

'Better do as she says,' Gino advised. 'Otherwise I'll
get to work on you myself.'

Neither of them had seen him come into the coffee
shop. Montelli scowled and withdrew his hand.

'Shall I thump him for you anyway?' Gino asked her
pleasantly.

'Don't you dare!' she said firmly. 'If there's any
thumping to be done I want the pleasure of doing it per-
sonally.'

Gino grinned. Then, glancing at Montelli, he said
curtly, 'Take yourself off.'

The transformation in him was astonishing. Instead of
the smiling boy there was a hard, steely man. Then it was
over, and the pleasant young man was there again. But

for a moment Alex could see that this was Rinaldo's brother.

Montelli saw it too, for he scuttled away.

'My chance to rescue a damsel in distress,' Gino said, laughing. 'And you had to spoil it. Couldn't you have pretended to be just a little bit scared for the sake of my male ego?'

'Oh, I should think your male ego is in fine healthy shape, without me buttering it up,' Alex observed, laughing with him.

'*Signorina*, you understand me perfectly,' he said.

He said 'signorina' differently to his brother, she thought, softer, almost with a caress, not grim and accusing. A natural flirt. A merry, uncomplicated lad. He would be excellent company.

'Are you going out?' he asked.

'Yes, I thought I'd do some sightseeing. I've never been to Florence before.'

'May I show you around? I'm at your service.'

'That would be nice. Let's have a coffee and discuss it.'

They found a small café near the loggia and drank coffee in sight of the bronze boar. Alex waited for him to tell her about the superstition of rubbing the beast's nose, but he did not.

But of course, she thought, *you know all about your brother's visit to me last night, how we fought, and then came here. He told you everything. This meeting was no accident.*

She smiled at Gino over the rim of her coffee cup, while her mind pursued her own thoughts.

He told you to come and find me, to see if charm worked any better than growling. Well, you are delight-

ful, my friend, and I'm happy to spend the day with you. But you don't fool me for a moment.

'Did Montelli hurt you, grabbing you like that?' Gino asked, taking her arm gently and studying it as though looking for bruises.

She barely felt his light touch. Nor could she recall the feel of Montelli's hand, unpleasant though it had been. The grasp that lingered was Rinaldo's, from the night before. Strange, she thought, how she could still feel that.

For a moment she saw his face again, intent, deadly, ready to do something desperate at any hint of a threat to what was his.

'No, Montelli didn't hurt me,' she said.

Gino held onto her just a little longer than necessary, before dropping her hand and saying, 'Let me take you to the Uffizi Gallery first. Here in Florence we have the greatest art in the world.'

Together they went around the vast gallery. Alex tried to look at all the pictures and show a proper appreciation, but it was too much for her. She felt as though great art was pursuing and attacking her.

They had lunch at a little restaurant overlooking the River Arno, with a perfect view of the Ponte Vecchio.

'I can't stop looking at the bridge,' Alex marvelled. 'All those buildings crowded onto it, making it seem so top-heavy. I keep thinking that it'll collapse into the water, but it doesn't. It's miraculous.'

'True,' Gino agreed. 'But then, all Florence is miraculous. Sixty per cent of the great art in the world is in Italy, and fifty per cent of that is in Florence. Because for the last few centuries—'

Alex hardly heard what he was saying. She was fascinated by him. Where else, she wondered, would a farmer lecture her about art?

But this was Florence, home of the Renaissance, which had produced men who were many sided, with subtle, wide-ranging minds.

'I'm sorry,' he said suddenly. 'Am I becoming a bore?'

'Not at all. You made me think of Renaissance man. I guess he's still around all these generations later.'

'Of course. That is our pride. Not that Rinaldo thinks so. He never raises his head from the land. But I think a man should have the soul of an artist even if he does get his hands dirty.'

She smiled, wondering exactly how dirty Gino's hands ever were. With Rinaldo she could believe it. He seemed to be a part of the very earth itself.

Gino regarded her sympathetically. 'I had thought to show you the Duomo after lunch, but—'

'Could we do that another time?' she begged. 'I couldn't cope with a cathedral just now.'

'Fine, let's find something less virtuous but far more fun.'

'Such as what?' she asked, eyeing him suspiciously.

'Horse riding?' he asked innocently. 'Why, what did you think I meant?'

Her lips twitched. 'Never mind. I'd love to go riding.'

Gino's glance met hers. His eyes flashed with humour, seeming to say that, yes, he'd been thinking exactly what she thought he was thinking. But that could come later.

Since she had no riding clothes a quick shopping trip was necessary. Gino had a nice eye for women's fashion, and refused to let her make a final choice until he had approved it.

At last, when she was wearing olive green trousers and a cream shirt, he nodded, saying, 'Perfect with your colouring. That's the one.'

While she paid he fetched his car to the shop. In a few

minutes they were on their way out of Florence, leading north to the hills.

At a small livery stable Gino hired a couple of horses, and they set off over the countryside. Alex was soon at home on the unfamiliar mare, who had a sweet disposition and a soft mouth.

After a good gallop they stopped in a village. The local inn had a garden, and they sat there eating fresh-baked bread and strong cheese.

'I love riding, but I haven't done any for a while,' Alex said with a sigh. 'This is wonderful.'

For the first time in days she felt totally relaxed and contented. The wildness of the scenery was alien to her, yet somehow it made her feel good.

David, she was sure, would never feel at ease here. His riding was done in the extensive grounds of his country house, on elegant animals from his own stables.

She realised suddenly that she hadn't spoken to him since she arrived. When she'd called his mobile phone had been switched off, so she had left a message.

She reached into her jacket pocket and checked her own phone, finding that it too was off. She wondered when she had done that.

She found a message from David to say that he'd called her back but been unable to get through. She dialled and found herself talking to his answering machine. After leaving a message she switched off again, returned the phone to her jacket, and looked up to find Gino watching her.

'Is he your lover?' he asked.

'What?'

'I'm sorry, I had no right to ask. But it's important to me to know.'

'You just want to know if I'm going to bring reinforcements out here?'

Gino shook his head. 'No, that's not what I meant. I have other reasons.'

His eyes told her what those reasons were. Alex did not speak. She wasn't sure what she would have said about David right now.

'You're like Rinaldo,' Gino said. 'He plays his cards close to his chest too.'

'Don't you dare say I'm like him!' she cried in mock indignation. 'He has no manners, and he acts like a juggernaut.'

'He really got under your skin last night, didn't he?'

'So he told you that? And how much of this meeting will you tell him about?'

She was teasing and he answered in the same vein. 'Not all of it.'

'Make sure he knows that I can be a juggernaut too.'

'I'll bet you made it plain to him yourself.'

She laughed. 'Come to think of it, yes I did.'

'You've got a lot of power, and he doesn't like other people having power, especially over him.'

'Well, it'll all be sorted out soon.'

'But how? You want your money.'

'Hey, there's no need to make me sound mercenary— even if Rinaldo thinks I am.'

'Sorry. I didn't mean it that way. But if we can't raise the money soon there'll be plenty who can, not just Montelli. Have any of the others approached you?'

Alex regarded him with her head on one side.

'Gino,' she teased, 'why don't you just tell Rinaldo not to treat me like a fool? Say you've had a wasted day.'

Gino's eyes gleamed.

'But the day isn't over yet. And, though you may not

believe it, the mortgage seems less important by the minute. There are so many other things about you that matter more.'

She gave him a smiling glance, but didn't answer in words.

They rode quietly back to the stables in the setting sun. Gino said little as he drove her back to Florence, but as he drew up outside the hotel he said, 'May I take you to dinner tonight?'

She couldn't resist saying, 'To make sure that nobody else does?'

He smiled and shook his head. 'No,' he said simply. 'Not for that reason.'

She just stopped herself from saying, 'And pigs fly!' He was a nice lad, and she was going to enjoy flirting the evening away with him. It would be different if she were fooled by his caressing ways, but she wasn't. Her heart was safe, and so, she was sure, was his.

There would be no disloyalty to David, and she might learn something useful in the coming battle.

'I'll believe you,' she teased. 'Thousands wouldn't.'

They settled that he would collect her at eight o'clock, which gave her time to find something to wear. She had thought herself well equipped with clothes, but the hotel's shopping arcade had a boutique with the latest lines from Milan.

With leisure to steep herself in Italian fashion she discovered it was unlike anything she had known before. She stepped into the shop, telling herself that she would just take a quick look. When she stepped out again she was the proud owner of a dark blue silk dress, demure in the front and low in the back, clinging on the hips.

His eyebrows went up when he saw her in the daring dress, complete with diamond earrings.

'*Signorina*,' he said softly, 'to be seen with you is an honour.'

Alex couldn't help it. She burst out laughing.

'What?' he asked in comic dismay.

'I'm sorry,' she choked. 'But I can't keep a straight face when you start that ''signorina'' stuff. I wish you'd just call me Alex, and remember that you're far more appealing when you're not trying so hard.'

'Does that mean you do find me appealing sometimes?' he asked with comical pathos.

'Are you going to feed me, or are we going to stand here talking all night?' she asked severely.

'I'm going to feed you,' he said hastily. 'I've booked us a table in a place very near here. Can you walk in those shoes?'

Her long legs ended in delicate silver sandals, with high heels.

'Of course I can,' she told him. 'It's just a question of balance.' She added significantly, 'And I'm very good at doing a balancing act.'

It was a perfect evening as they strolled down to the banks of the Arno and across the Ponte Vecchio. Alex paused to look into the shops that lined the bridge. There had been goldsmiths here for centuries, and their wares were still displayed in gorgeous profusion.

As at lunchtime, they ate near the river. Now the daylight was fading, the lamps were coming on, reflected in the water, and there was a new kind of magic.

Gino was also a perfect host, surrounding her with a cocoon of comfort and consideration, entertaining her with funny stories.

She made him talk about the farm and his life there, while she ate her way through chicken liver canapés, noodles with hare sauce, and *Bistecca al la Fiorentina*, a charbroiled steak.

'It's been cooked this way since the fourteenth century,' Gino explained. 'The legend says that the town magistrates used to cook it themselves in the Palazzo Vecchio, if it was a busy day. It saved going home for lunch.'

'You made that up.'

'I swear I didn't. I don't say that it's true, but it's the legend.'

'And a good legend can be as powerful as the truth,' Alex mused.

He nodded. 'More. Because the legend tells you what people *want* to believe.'

She gave a little laugh. 'Like your brother wants to believe in me as a Wicked Witch.'

Gino regarded her wryly. 'Do you know how often you do that?' he asked.

'Do what?'

'Bring the conversation back to Rinaldo. You've convinced yourself that he's pulling my strings, and I feel as though you don't really see me at all. You're looking over my shoulder at him all the time.'

'I'm sorry,' she said quickly. 'I didn't mean to sound like that. It's just—well, perhaps you should blame him. I'm sure he likes to think of himself as pulling your strings—everyone's strings. Somehow, one takes him at his own estimation.'

'That's true,' he said with a rueful sigh. 'Let's have some champagne.'

He turned to call the waiter, leaving Alex to reflect. She was shaken by the realisation that Gino was right. While she smiled and flirted with him, Rinaldo seemed to be constantly there, an unseen but dominant presence.

When the champagne had arrived he began to reminisce once more about his childhood.

'I'll never forget the day my father brought me to Florence for the carnival in the streets. We went through it together, visiting all the stalls. He was as much a kid as I was. At least, that's what my mother always said.'

'How old were you when she died?'

'Eight.'

'How sad! And your father never remarried?'

'No, he said he never would, and he stuck to that until his own death.'

'Your father sounds like a delightful person,' she said warmly.

'He was. Of course, Rinaldo thought he was too frivolous, always joking when he should have been serious. Poppa would tease him and say, "Lighten up, the world is a better place than you think".'

'Now you're doing it,' she told him. 'Bringing the conversation back to Rinaldo.'

'I know. As you say, it's hard not to.'

'What did he used to say when your father teased him like that?'

'Nothing, he'd just scowl and remember something that had to be done somewhere else. I'll swear nothing matters to him but work.'

'Well, I suppose that's good in a way,' Alex said. 'The work has to be done.'

'Hey, I do my share. It's just that, like Poppa, I believe in having fun too.'

'Has Rinaldo always been gloomy?'

'He's always been serious, but it's really only since his wife died that he's actually been morose.'

'His wife?' Alex echoed, startled.

'Yes, her name was Maria. She came from Fiesole, a

tiny little town near here. They were childhood sweet-hearts. I think they got engaged when they were fifteen. They married when they were twenty.'

'What was she like?' Alex asked curiously.

She was trying to imagine the kind of woman who would attract Rinaldo, but she found it hard to picture him in love.

'She was pretty and plump and motherly. You'd prob-ably call her old-fashioned because all she wanted was to look after us. My mother was dead by then, so it was really nice having her.'

'Is that why he married her?' Alex asked, scandalised. 'To have a woman about the place?'

Gino grinned.

'Oh no! He was crazy about her. It was Poppa and me who needed motherly attention. I was ten years old. Maria was a great cook, and that's really all a ten-year-old boy cares about. She and Rinaldo seemed very happy. I used to see him come up behind her, put his arms about her and nuzzle her neck. He was a changed man. He laughed.'

'What happened?'

'They were going to have a baby, but it was born at seven months and both mother and child died.'

'Oh, heavens!' Alex whispered in horror. 'How long ago was that?'

'Fifteen years. They'd been married for less than two years.'

'How awful for him. To be so young and watch his wife die—'

'It was worse than that. He wasn't there. Nobody ex-pected the baby to come so soon, and he was away buy-ing machinery. Poppa called him as soon as things started to happen and he rushed back, but he was too late.

'I was there in the hospital when he arrived, and I'll never forget the sight of him. He'd driven all night, and he looked like a madman, with wild eyes. When the doctor told him Maria was dead he wouldn't believe it. He rushed into her room and seized her up in his arms.

'I'd never seen him cry before. I didn't think it was possible, but he was off his head.

'At that stage the baby was still alive, but not expected to live. They baptised him quickly. He wanted to hold him, but he couldn't because he had to stay in the incubator. It was no use though. He died half an hour later.

'By that time he'd calmed down but it was almost worse than when he was raving. He was in a trance, just staring and not seeing anything. He got through the funeral like that—just one funeral, with them both in the same coffin. It was almost as though he didn't know what was happening.

'Since then he never speaks of them. If I try to mention them he just blanks me out. I'm not sure what he feels now. Probably nothing. He seems to have deadened that side of him.'

'Can any man do that?' Alex mused.

'Rinaldo can. He can do whatever he sets his mind to. Why should he want to go through such pain again?'

'But surely it could never happen again? No man could be so unlucky twice.'

'I think he's decided not to take a chance on it. Since Maria died the farm has been his whole life. Poppa left the running of it to him.'

'What about you?'

Gino gave his attractive boyish grin.

'Theoretically I have as much authority as my brother, but Rinaldo's a great one for letting you know who's the meat and who's the potatoes. His being so much older helps, of course.'

There was something slightly mechanical about Alex's smile. She no longer felt able to joke about Rinaldo. The image of the overbearing dictator that had dominated her thoughts had suddenly become blurred.

There was another image now, a young man agonising over the death of his wife and child, then growing older too fast, hardening in his despair.

'Are you all right?' Gino asked as she rubbed her hand over her eyes.

'Yes, I'm just a little tired. I'm not used to so much heat.'

'Let me take you back to the hotel.'

The night air was blessedly cool as they strolled back. To her relief he seemed in tune with her mood, and did not talk.

At the door of the hotel he took her hand and said, 'I'd ask to see you again, but you'd only think Rinaldo put me up to it. So I won't.'

She smiled. 'That's very clever.'

'But it's all right if I call you, isn't it?'

'Yes, but not tomorrow.'

He nodded. Leaning forward he kissed her cheek gently, and walked away.

Gino slipped into the house quietly, but his caution was wasted, as he had feared that it would be.

'Good evening,' Rinaldo said, without looking up from the computer screen where he was doing the accounts.

'Don't you ever sleep?' Gino asked.

Rinaldo didn't answer this. Dragging his eyes away from the screen he leaned back, stretching like a man whose limbs had been cramped too long.

'You look like the cat that swallowed the cream,' he observed. 'I hope the cream was good.'

'Don't be coarse.'

'I also hope you didn't forget that you were there for a purpose. You haven't just been enjoying yourself, you were supposed to be neutralising a threat.'

'Alex is no threat. She's trying to be as helpful to us as she can.'

Rinaldo groaned.

'She really got to you, didn't she? Well, before you get too starry-eyed, remember that this is the woman who was negotiating with Montelli at our father's funeral.'

'She wasn't negotiating. He just walked up to her. In fact he did it again today and she drove him off with threats of violence. I heard her.'

'He was there again?'

'They were in the coffee shop when I arrived, and she sent him packing.'

'Of course—because she saw you.'

'You're a cynical swine, aren't you?'

'I know more about women than you do, and a damned sight more about hard cash. And one of us needs to be cynical about this lady. You're evidently a lost cause. What did she do? Flutter her eyelids and let you look deep into her blue eyes?'

'They're not exactly blue,' Gino said, considering. 'More like a kind of violet.'

'They looked ordinary blue to me.'

'Maybe you weren't looking at them in the right way.'

'I was looking at them with suspicion, and that's the right way,' Rinaldo growled.

'Well, maybe it was the dress,' Gino agreed. 'That was dark blue and very elegant, sort of clingy, especially over her waist and hips—'

Rinaldo got to his feet restively.

'I don't want to hear any more,' he growled. 'You've plainly made a fool of yourself—'

'If you mean that I'm enchanted, I plead guilty.'

'Enchanted. Listen to yourself. You were sent on a mission and you return spouting a lot of sentimental drivel. She's probably laughing at you this minute. In fact, it wouldn't surprise me if she got straight on the phone to Montelli as soon as you left.'

'You're determined to think the worst of her, aren't you?'

'With reason.'

'You know nothing about her,' Gino said with a flash of anger. 'You've been prejudiced since the first moment.'

'Do you blame me?'

'I blame you for not giving her a chance.'

Rinaldo sighed.

'But it isn't up to me. It lies in her hands now, that's what's so damned—' he checked himself.

'Don't worry,' Gino said. 'She's as crazy about me as I am about her. From now on, everything's going to be fine.'

CHAPTER FOUR

ALEX had often heard of the magic of Italy, but, being a practical person, she had dismissed it as romanticising. Now she found that it was real.

Perhaps it was in the light that intensified every colour. Or perhaps it was Florence, packed with medieval buildings, where there were as many cobblestones as modern roads.

She tried not to be seduced by the beauty. She was only here to raise money, then return to London, marriage to David, the partnership: in other words, her 'real' life.

It was just that it seemed less real suddenly, and she could feel no hurry to push things along. David had told her to take as much time as she needed, and it might be better to stay here for a while, and broaden her mind.

So the day after her meeting with Gino, she did something she hadn't done for years. She played hookey.

Firmly turning off her mobile phone she hired a car and left Florence, heading south. After a few miles she began to climb until she reached the tiny, ancient town of Fiesole.

After wandering its cobbled streets for an hour, she found a restaurant with tables on a balcony looking far down, and sat there, sipping coffee and gazing at the rows of cypresses, and the elegant villas that were laid out before her.

'You're in good company,' said a quiet voice.

Rinaldo had appeared, seemingly from nowhere. She

wondered how long he had been standing there, watching her.

But today, although his face was grave, there was no antagonism in it as he came to sit at her table.

'Good company?' she asked.

'Your English writers, Shelley and Dickens, once admired this valley. Down there is the villa where Lorenzo de Medici entertained his literary friends. This little town is known as the mother of Florence. Look around and you'll see why.'

Alex saw it at once. The whole panorama of Florence, barely five miles away, was spread out before them, glowing in the noon haze, the great Duomo rising out of a sea of roofs, dwarfing everything else.

'What are you doing up here?' he asked lightly.

'Do I need your permission?'

'Not at all, but wouldn't you be better occupied negotiating? You're a woman of business. There's work to be done, and here you are, wasting time, staring into the distance.'

Alex didn't normally quote poetry, but this time she couldn't resist it.

'What is this life if, full of care,

We have no time to stand and stare?'

Rinaldo frowned. 'Who said that?'

'An English poet.'

'An *Englishman?*' he demanded on an unflattering emphasis.

'Yes,' she said, nettled. 'Strange as it may seem, an Englishman wrote it. Shock! Horror! Now you might have to adjust your ideas about the English.

'You think of me holding court, receiving my financial suitors one by one, selling you out to the highest bidder. And let's face it, that's how you prefer to see me.'

Rinaldo hailed a passing waiter and ordered two coffees. Alex had an amused feeling that he was giving himself a breathing space to come to terms with her attack.

'You were probably following me up here,' she added,
'to see if I met up with a prospective buyer behind your
back.'

'No, I've been visiting friends in Fiesole. This is pure
chance.'

Suddenly she remembered that Gino had said his wife
came from this town, and wondered if he had been to see
Maria's family.

'Anyway, you're wrong,' she said in a gentler tone. 'I
have nothing to negotiate, not with Montelli or anyone
else of his kind, until I've first talked seriously with you.
Anyway, I dislike him.'

Rinaldo gave her a grin that was as harsh as it was
humorous. 'The question is, do you dislike him as much
as you dislike me?'

'I haven't quite decided, but it makes no difference. I
never allow personalities to interfere with business.'

'Like a good accountant?' he mocked.

'No, like a civilised human being actually,' she said
crisply.

He gave a half nod, acknowledging a hit to her.

The coffees were served, giving them both a brief time
out.

'I wonder what your notion of "civilised" includes,'
he mused when they were alone again. 'My brother?'

'Your brother is a nice lad, but I told him, and I'm
telling you, don't treat me like a fool.'

'Meaning?'

'Meaning that you should have been ashamed to be so
obvious. You sent him out to say pretty nothings to me
because you thought I was a ninny who'd faint the mo-

ment an Italian gave her the eye. Well, he's delightful and he made my head spin—not perhaps as much as you planned, but enough for a very nice day.

'But let me make one thing plain to you, Signor Farnese. I do not make serious decisions while my head is spinning. I hope that's clear.'

He began to laugh, a robust, virile sound that was free from strain. He could be really attractive, she realised; a man, in contrast to his brother's boyishness.

'I see that Gino has been fooling himself,' he said. 'This isn't the impression I got from him.'

There was a silence, during which they eyed each other. Alex smiled.

'Signor Farnese, if you're waiting for me to ask what he said about me, you'll wait for ever.'

He raised his eyebrows. 'You're not interested in knowing?'

'Let's just say that I have exceptional self-control.'

He inclined his head in salute.

'My compliments, *signorina*. You fight with courage and skill. Poor Gino. I'm afraid you'll break his heart.'

'I don't think there's any fear of that! He knew the nature of the duel. His heart isn't involved any more than mine.'

'Don't be too sure of that. Gino is a man who gives his affections easily. In that, he is not like me, or you.'

'You know nothing about me.'

'Only what you've just told me, which is that you're a woman who likes to be in control—'

'Just like you.'

'Just like me. Also like me, your head rules your heart. I respect that, but it makes me wary of you.'

'You mean I'm not going to be the simple-minded walkover that you were expecting.'

'I don't think I would ever call you simple-minded,' he said gravely. 'May I buy you lunch?'

'No, thank you. I've had a snack and it's time for me to be going.'

'Let me walk with you to your car.'

She led the short distance to where she had parked, and as soon as he saw her car he grimaced.

'What's wrong?' she demanded.

'I know this car. I know the firm you hired it from. Neither are reliable.'

As if to prove it, the car made forlorn choking noises and refused to budge.

'Oh, great!' she said, exasperated. 'How do I start this?'

'You don't. You'll have to abandon it and tell the firm to come for it later.'

Muttering, she got out and called the hire firm on her mobile phone. The ensuing conversation was terse on both sides. The firm was reluctant to accept responsibility, insisting that the car had been perfect when consigned to her, and that it was her job to get it back.

As the argument grew heated she saw, to her annoyance, that Rinaldo was observing and taking in everything. At last, with the air of a man who could endure no more, he reached over, took the phone from her and spoke into it sharply and in Tuscan.

The effect was instantaneous. As she recovered the phone and put it to her ear the man on the other end was burbling with eagerness to please. Alex couldn't decide whether she was more relieved to have the business sorted, or exasperated at being beholden to Rinaldo. His grin told her that he understood her dilemma perfectly.

'Thank you,' she said crisply. 'I'm grateful to you.'

'No you're not,' he said cheerfully. 'You'd like to murder me.'

'I'm far too much of a lady to say so.'

The phone rang before she could switch it off. She answered, turning away slightly.

'Alex?' It was David's voice.

'Hello, darling.'

'I got your message. Sorry I couldn't call back before. How are you doing out there?'

'It has its ups and downs.'

'I take it the arrangements are problematic?'

'Very,' she said. 'But I'll get there.'

'Are the Farnese brothers being difficult?'

'Nothing I can't cope with,' she said, loud enough for Rinaldo to hear.

'Don't stand for it,' David told her. 'You hold all the cards.'

'Well, I know that. But everything isn't as simple as it seemed when we were talking in England.'

'If they start making themselves unpleasant, just set the lawyers onto them.'

'It's sweet of you to worry about me,' she said tenderly, 'but honestly darling, I'm coping really well.'

'Hm! Well, I suppose that's true. I know how efficient you always are.'

Alex made a wry face. As a tribute 'efficient' lacked something. But David had never been a man for emotional pronouncements. Once she had liked that about him. Now it struck a jarring note.

'Just leave everything to me,' she said.

He laughed suddenly. 'I begin to feel sorry for them. They don't know what they've taken on.'

She joined in his laughter, but she would have preferred to hear it put some other way.

'Take as long as you need,' David said. 'I've got your work here covered so you don't need to give it another thought.'

'Thank you, but of course I think about it all the time. And you. It'll be lovely getting back to you.'

'We're going to have a lot to talk about,' he assured her.

Rinaldo heard her laughter and it chilled him. Without consciously eavesdropping—so he told himself—he had contrived to hear enough to alarm him.

This man was a lover, in her thoughts all the time. She called him 'darling' and longed to return to him.

He began to appreciate the true dimensions of the threat to everything he held dear, and he called himself a fool for underestimating the danger.

His eyes narrowed as he came to a swift resolution. Alex was hanging up, turning back to him, and he swung away from her so that she shouldn't see his thoughts reflected in his face.

When he was ready to face her again he was smiling.

'Come,' he said, taking her hand. 'This way to my car.'

'I can't go with you. I have to stay here for the breakdown truck.'

'Nonsense. Just leave the keys in the ignition. Nobody can steal it, since the car can't move. Now come on.'

He was making his way to a car on the far side of the parking lot.

'Come where?' she asked.

She tried to pull away but his grip, although light, was unbreakable.

'There are things you need to see.'

'Will you let me go?'

'No, I won't. So don't waste time asking me.'

'This is kidnap,' she seethed.

'You can call it what you like.'

It would have been easy to scream for help, and rouse some passer-by to assist her. Alex could never quite understand why she didn't do this.

She was still considering the matter as he opened the door of his vehicle for her to get in.

The car was a heavy four-wheel drive, long past its best, but suitable for rough terrain. Swinging out of Fiesole they were soon at the bottom of the slope and heading for the great hills she could see looming ahead, waiting for them.

'Are you going to show me Belluna?' she asked.

'Some of it. There's too much to see in one go. But it's time you saw what you're negotiating about.'

Soon they began to climb again. Florence vanished. The land grew wild, fierce, somehow darker, yet filled with violent colour. Had there ever been such colours, she wondered?

'Stop a moment,' she said.

Rinaldo halted the car, and she immediately opened the door and jumped out.

'Careful!' he cried. 'It's steep here. But you picked a good place.'

They were up high, looking far out over the valley and the far hills. The sun streamed down over the scene, touching fields, full of flourishing crops. Far off there was a village, its red roofs and glinting windows also bathed in warmth and light.

Alex took a deep breath, filling her lungs with the pure fresh air, without a trace of city fumes.

She was city born and bred, and had always regarded London as her natural home. But in these wide spaces she suddenly felt free to breathe, as if for the first time.

'Over there are the vineyards,' Rinaldo said, coming

beside her. 'See, on that steep slope, with the vines arranged in tiers so that they all catch as much of the sun as possible.

'We also grow wheat and olives, but I dare say the lawyers have told you all that.'

'I've seen it all written down in columns,' she agreed. 'But this—is so different.'

'This is just cash to you, but to us the land is a living, breathing creature that works with us to create new life. Then again, sometimes it works against us, even tries to kill us. But it belongs to us, as we belong to it.'

She mopped her brow. It was the hottest part of the day.

'Come over here,' he said, taking her arm and leading her to where a stream plunged downhill. There were a few trees in this spot, giving a blessed shade.

'Maybe I shouldn't have brought you here just now,' he said. 'You're not used to this kind of heat.'

'I'm very tough,' she assured him.

'You don't look it. You look as if a breeze would blow you away.'

She laughed and made a gesture to indicate the still air. 'What breeze?'

'Sit down,' he said, urging her to the water's edge.

His own face and neck were damp with perspiration. He pulled out a clean handkerchief and dropped it into the stream, then squeezing the water over himself. Alex tried to do the same, but her handkerchief was too small to be effective.

'Here,' he said, soaking his again and passing it to her.

She buried her face in it, grateful for the relief, then drenched it again. When she had finished she found him looking at her.

She guessed he was watching for some sign of weakness. If so, he would be disappointed. She had her second wind now and knew that this was something she could deal with, even relish. The sheer ferocity of the elements in this country had lit a small flame of excitement in her. Go now, warned a voice in her head. Before it grows and takes you over.

She laid her hand against the earth, moving her fingers to feel it against her.

'Not like that,' he said quietly. 'Dig in deep, and really feel it. Let it speak to you.'

She tried it, and knew at once what he meant. Here by the stream the earth was springy, damp and crumbling. From it came a lush, powerful odour that was not unpleasant.

Speaking almost in a daze she said, 'You could grow anything in this.'

His answer came without words. Plunging his own hand into the ground he raised it to show her. She touched it, and at once he gripped her hand, pressing it into the rich earth that he was holding.

It felt good, and the sense of power in his hands beneath the living soil made her strangely giddy.

'You see?' he said intently. 'You see?'

'Yes,' she whispered. 'I see.'

Something seemed to have taken possession of her. She didn't want to open her fingers. She had the impression that the sun had darkened, but instead of blotting out her surroundings it made them more vivid.

There was a big scar on the back of his hand. She couldn't take her eyes away from it.

Then he moved, prising her fingers open and drawing her hand gently down into the cleansing water.

'It's time we were going,' he said quietly.

She nodded, rubbing the earth away, past speech.

When she was sitting beside him in the car he turned it and began the journey back down the track to where the road forked. There was a signpost, showing the way to Florence, but he swung away.

'Where are we going?' she asked.

'I'm taking you home.'

'Home?'

'My home.'

She didn't let him see how much this pleased her. She was more curious to see Rinaldo's home than she would admit.

She had pictured a shabby, weather-beaten farmhouse, but the building that finally came into view had a touch of grandeur. It was three stories high, with a double staircase that formed two curves up the front.

But what really amazed her was that it was made of a stone that appeared pink in the red-gold of the setting sun. At that moment the sun shone directly into her eyes, making her blink, and giving the building the appearance of a frosted cake.

She blinked again and the world righted itself. It was just a house, although still more ornate than any farmhouse she had ever seen.

'It's beautiful,' she breathed.

'Yes,' he agreed. 'At one time it was what I supposed you'd call a great house, but the man who owned it two hundred years ago fell on hard times. He had to sell off some of his land, and start farming the rest.

'The place has changed hands several times. My grandfather bought it and worked himself into the grave to make it prosper. My father gave his whole life to it as well.'

'And you live in that beautiful house?'

'Part of it. The rest is shut up. Teresa, who looks after

us, complains about how hard it is to keep even a small part clean.'

A door at ground level was pulled open from the inside, but, instead of Teresa, Alex saw a vast dog, of miscellaneous parentage, come lumbering out.

He might have been part Great Dane, part Alsatian. He might have been a St Bernard crossed with a lurcher. He might have been anything.

He ambled towards them obviously so excited to see them that he was getting dangerously near the vehicle. Rinaldo was forced to brake sharply.

A stream of fierce words came from him. The dog either didn't understand or didn't care because he reared up to put his head through Rinaldo's window and cover him with eager licks.

'That's enough,' Rinaldo growled, but he didn't push the animal away. 'This ridiculous object is Brutus,' he informed Alex. 'He thinks he's mine. Or I'm his. One of the two.'

He tweaked the animal's ears and said, *'Vai via!'* pointing into the distance.

Reluctantly Brutus moved back. But as soon as they were out of the car he surged forward again, this time at Alex.

She gave a yell of alarm. The next moment she was looking down at her elegant pants, now displaying a large, dirty paw print.

She opened her mouth, but her exclamation was checked by the sight of the dog, beaming at her, clearly convinced that he had done something brilliant.

'It would be a waste of time saying anything to you, wouldn't it?' she demanded, pointing to the smudge.

He woofed agreement.

'Then I won't bother,' she said, smiling despite herself. 'But if you do it again—'

He waited, grinning foolishly.

'If you do it again—' she sighed, recognising defeat '—then I guess I'll just have to forgive you again.'

Ecstatic at this appreciation, Brutus reared up and placed another mark next to the first.

'My apologies,' Rinaldo said, sounding strained. *'Brutus!'*

'Oh, don't be mad at him,' Alex said. 'He was only being friendly. I suppose he's made that way.'

'No, he doesn't usually take to strangers. He's never done that before. Naturally I'll pay the cost of cleaning.'

Alex shook her head. The sight of Rinaldo at a disadvantage was improving her mood.

'I shouldn't bother,' she said. 'It won't clean.'

'Then I will pay for a replacement,' he said stiffly.

Alex began to laugh. 'Don't force me to tell you how much it cost,' she said. 'I don't want to spoil your supper.'

He regarded her oddly. 'You're being very nice about it.'

'And that's really got you puzzled, hasn't it? If I'm being nice, it must be for an evil purpose. Forget it for heaven's sake! A dog is a dog is a dog. Making a mess is what dogs do.'

Now she had really wrong-footed him, she saw with pleasure. He was no longer quite so certain what to think of her, and that confused him.

Good! The longer she could keep him confused the better.

Teresa appeared. She was elderly, with white hair and sharp blue eyes that flickered quickly over Alex.

'Teresa, this is Signorina Dacre, from England. Enrico Mori was her great-uncle.'

'Buon giorno, signorina.'

'Buon giorno, Teresa,' Alex responded.

He introduced Alex, who saw the briefest reaction flicker across the housekeeper's face. She wondered how freely the brothers had discussed her, and what Teresa had overheard.

'Let's go inside,' Rinaldo said. 'The *signorina* has been out in the heat for too long. Show her to the guest room, please, Teresa.'

The walls of the house were thick enough to keep out the heat. The old-fashioned room was blessedly cool, and half an hour was enough to restore Alex to herself. She was feeling cheerful as she went downstairs to be shown into a room at the back of the house.

At the far end were tall windows that opened onto a veranda. A table stood just outside the room, laden with small snacks. Rinaldo was there. He looked up as she entered.

'Are you feeling better?' he asked pleasantly.

'Yes thank you. Mind you, I never did feel actually bad, just—a little overwhelmed. It was suddenly so—'

She found that she couldn't finish. No words were adequate.

Rinaldo nodded without speaking, and she knew that he understood everything she was trying to say.

He poured her a glass of light *prosecco* wine, and she sipped, glad to find it ice-cold.

Now the weather was cooling and they could sit on the veranda, while Teresa served them a sweet, crusted pie with macaroni and meat sauce, which he told her was called *Pasticcio alla Fiorentina.*

'Are you wise to treat me like this?' she teased. 'You might make me want to stay.'

'What about the man who called you? Isn't he yearning for you to return?'

She gave a choke of laughter. There was something about the idea of David yearning that was irresistibly comic.

'What is it?' he asked, watching her.

'David isn't like that. Yearning isn't his way.'

'What is his way?'

'Well—I don't know—'

'But you're in love with him?'

'Yes—no—it's none of your business.'

'As long as I'm in your power, everything about you is my business.'

'I see no need to discuss David.'

'Is he a painful subject?'

'No, he isn't. It's just that our relationship is—difficult to describe—'

'You mean it isn't passionate,' he said calmly.

'I mean nothing of the kind.'

'Then it is passionate? His kisses inflame you, your body aches for him when you are apart?'

Alex's lips twitched. Her sense of humour was coming to her rescue.

'You forget,' she said, 'that I'm a cold-blooded northerner. We don't "do" passion. It gets in the way of business.'

His eyes gleamed. 'A remark like that is pure provocation.'

'You can take it any way you like. David is the man I'm going to marry, and I refuse to discuss our relationship any further.'

He was silent for a long moment after that. Alex knew

that the announcement of her impending marriage was like a glove thrown down in defiance, warning him that she had her own agenda. But his face was slightly averted, and she couldn't discern what effect it had had on him.

At last he raised his head and spoke.

'Teresa is ready to serve the next course. I hope you're hungry.'

CHAPTER FIVE

TERESA served game bird cooked with Marsala wine and juniper berries. It was delicious and Alex soon persuaded herself that arguments could wait.

Sitting on the veranda they could see the light fade from the land and the sun turn deep red before sliding down the sky. Here and there a cloud seemed lit by crimson from behind.

Brutus moved between them, begging. To Alex's surprise Rinaldo showed no impatience, but fed the old dog patiently, although he advised her, 'Don't let him pester you.'

'I don't mind being pestered,' Alex said with perfect truth. 'He's beautiful.'

'He's a dog,' Rinaldo said with a touch of curtness. 'Come on, boy.'

He pushed his chair back abruptly and went into the house, calling Brutus, who followed docilely. Alex wondered about his sudden change of mood, as though she had offended him by petting his dog.

But when he returned a few moments later he seemed to have forgotten the matter.

'It's good that we have a chance to talk,' he said. 'I understand your situation better now. So, you plan to marry this David, and that's why you need money.'

'No, I need it to buy my partnership in the firm,' she said. 'David's an accountant too. It's one of the top firms in London, so a partnership comes expensive.'

She waited for him to make some sharp remark, but he only nodded, as if considering.

'How well did you know Enrico?' he asked.

'Not well at all, although he was very fond of my mother, and she talked about him a lot. In fact she talked about Italy a lot. She told me so much about Tuscany that when I got here it was like coming to a place I'd always known. She even raised me to speak Italian as well as English.'

Rinaldo frowned as though trying to remember something.

'What was your mother's name?'

'Berta.'

'Was she short and dainty with reddish hair?'

'That's right. You knew her?'

'I met her once, years ago. Enrico brought her to a party here. I was about seven and she was grown up, but she was great fun. I had this dice game that I insisted on playing with everyone until they were ready to scream.

'She sat down with me and we played and played and played. She was a mean dice player, and she had a wonderful giggle. She beat me hollow. She went to England a couple of months later and I never saw her again. So you're Berta's daughter.'

'But you must always have known this?' Alex pointed it out.

'I suppose I did know it at the back of my mind, but it's only just come to the forefront. I must have been too angry to think straight.'

'Does that make me less of an enemy?'

He considered.

'Can you play dice?'

They both laughed.

'Tell me some more about her,' he said.

'Mamma was very hot-tempered and dramatic. We didn't understand each other but we loved each other. I think I'm beginning to understand her better now.'

'Already? You've only been here a few days.'

'I know. But it's not a matter of working it out in my head. It's something I'm breathing in with the air. How could anyone be cool, calm and collected in this place?'

Rinaldo nodded. 'You can't. And we're not.'

'Surely there must be some Italians who are moderate and reasonable?' Alex said in a teasing voice.

He smiled. 'There may be one or two, hiding in corners.'

'Probably ashamed to show their faces.'

'Undoubtedly. Italy was built on passion, not reason. Moderation didn't create those great buildings and great paintings that you've seen in Florence. Passion created them, and everything else worth having, food, wine, beauty—you will find none of these sitting behind a desk.'

'Meaning me. But isn't there also a kind of beauty in good order?'

She had expected him to brush this aside, but to her surprise he nodded.

'Yes,' he said. 'But not if it's the only thing in your life.'

She would have defended herself against this slur, but somehow the words wouldn't come. What came into her mind instead was the picture of herself at her desk, at her computer, hurrying from one meeting to another in a grey, air-conditioned building from which fresh air, and anything else that was natural, had been shut out.

And the carefully scheduled time with David. All part of her life's plan. Good order. But beauty?

The sun was throwing out its last fires of gold and

crimson, drifting slowly down the sky. Its glow fell on her, and on Rinaldo. She felt not only its warmth but a feeling of contentment.

It might be wiser to resist that feeling, she thought drowsily. But for the moment she had no will to resist.

Far off in the distance she could see something moving. After a moment she made out Gino's car, heading towards them, growing larger every moment.

When he was close to the house he waved before sweeping around to the side and vanishing.

She liked Gino, but at this moment she found herself wishing he had stayed away a little longer. He could only be an intrusion in the magical atmosphere that was pervading her.

How strange, she thought, that it should be Rinaldo who was here with her, part of the magic. The man who had shown her only his harsh, formidable side was now relaxed and pleasant.

To her relief, Gino didn't join them at once. Teresa served fruits in syrup followed by black, sweet coffee.

'Now here is beauty,' Alex agreed.

'I'll tell Teresa you said so. She will appreciate it.'

'I'll tell her myself, just before I leave.'

'Yes,' he said after a moment.

'I must be going soon, I suppose. I want an early night, to be ready for Enrico's funeral tomorrow. His family are making a big "do" of it.'

'Aren't you part of his family?'

'Well yes, but you know what I mean. The people who live out here and knew him. And let me tell you, *they* don't consider me as part of the family. They're as angry with me as you are.'

'I'm not angry with you, as I hope I've made clear today. Belluna has gained much prosperity from the

money my father borrowed, and it's your right to be re-
paid.'

Alex wrinkled her nose.

'I don't like talk of ''rights'',' she said, wondering at
herself even as she said it.

In the world she had left behind, the world of desks
and good order, rights were the markers by which everything was organised. You were entitled to this, you
weren't entitled to that. And so you always knew where
you stood in the universe.

But here the universe was a flood of gold spread over
the land. And rights seemed unimportant.

'I suppose Enrico's funeral will turn out the same way
your father's did,' she said. 'The vultures will converge
on me.'

'I think I have a way to prevent that happening,' Rinaldo mused.

Before she could ask what he meant Gino appeared,
greeting her eagerly, kissing her cheek.

'I'm so glad,' he said. 'When Rinaldo told me, I
couldn't believe it.'

'Told you what?'

'Why, that you'd come to stay, of course.'

'But I haven't come to stay. I'm about to return to
Florence, if someone will give me a lift.'

In the silence Gino looked at Rinaldo, who shrugged
with an air that was almost sheepish. At any other time
this would have amused her, but now a rising tide of
suspicion was overtaking her, making her get to her feet
to confront him.

'But I just finished bringing your bags,' Gino protested.

She whirled on him.

'And why would you do that?'

'Because Rinaldo said—hey, brother, you wouldn't! Would you?'

'Would you like to bet money on that?' Alex seethed.

'Look,' Rinaldo said, 'it's right for you to stay here awhile, and learn to understand this place.'

'OK. That makes sense. But why couldn't you have simply asked me?'

'You might have said no,' he declared flatly, as if the question were too obvious to need an answer.

'I *am* saying no. I absolutely refuse to stay here now.'

'But Teresa is in your room right now, unpacking your bags,' Gino said in dismay.

'And that's another thing,' Alex told him furiously. 'How did you come to have my luggage? I never packed it.'

'The hotel did that,' Gino said. 'They had everything ready for me.'

'And who told them to?'

Gino held up his hands, backing away as if to say that this wasn't his fault.

'I did,' Rinaldo said. 'I called them and said you weren't returning, and would they please have your things ready.'

'And did you pay my bill as well, or weren't they worried about that little matter?'

'You may recall that you signed a credit card docket when you arrived. It was simply a matter of putting it through. But I doubt if they would have worried anyway. The manager is an old friend of mine.'

'And would have jumped to obey your orders?' Alex said angrily.

Rinaldo shrugged. 'There was no need to give him orders. He knows I can be trusted. And, as I said, he already had your signature.'

'Suppose I want to dispute something on the bill?'

'You can do that tomorrow.'

'I'll do it now. I refuse to stay here. You must be quite mad.' She faced Gino, eyes glinting. 'I thought better of you.'

'But I didn't know, truly,' he pleaded. 'I thought you'd agreed.'

'Will you take me back to Florence? Or must I call for a taxi?'

'Of course I'll take you back,' he said at once.

'Forget that idea,' Rinaldo growled.

'I won't forget it,' Gino said firmly. 'Rinaldo, what are you thinking about?'

'I'm thinking about how all this is going to end,' he shouted.

'And making everyone dance around like puppets on the end of your strings,' Alex snapped. 'What did you think I'd do when I found out? Tamely submit to your decree and let you take me prisoner? If you did, you were wrong.'

'Take you prisoner? Don't be melodramatic.'

'What else would you call it?'

'*I'd* call it taking a lady prisoner,' Gino observed. 'Alex, I'll drive you back to Florence.'

At that defiance Rinaldo flung him a look that Alex never forgot. It contained rage, betrayal, disbelief, and a curious sense of hurt that she couldn't help seeing, even then.

'Gino,' Rinaldo warned, 'don't take anyone's side against me.'

'Then don't force a battle about this,' Gino said in a harsher voice than Alex had heard from him before. 'It's gone too far. You're always the same. You lose your temper and you forget everything else. Too many people jump to do as you say, but Alex doesn't. That's what's got you mad.'

Rinaldo didn't reply in words, but his look was terrible.

'Do as you like,' he said curtly.

Gino swung around to face Alex.

'I don't want you to leave,' he said quietly, 'but if that's your wish, I'm ready to take you back now.'

Alex put her hand in his.

'Do you really want me to stay?'

'More than anything, but not against your will.'

'Gino, I'm happy to remain here if I'm asked nicely and not steamrollered.'

He grinned and dropped to his knee, holding her hand between his.

'Alex, will you honour us by being our guest for as long as you wish?'

'I accept,' she said hastily, fearing that Rinaldo would explode if this went on. He was regarding them both with an air of grim exasperation.

'For pity's sake,' he snapped. 'If you mean to stay, what's the fuss about?'

'You really don't know, do you?' Alex demanded.

'No, he doesn't,' Gino confirmed.

Rinaldo scowled at him.

'If you gentlemen have finished,' Alex said, thoroughly fed up with both of them, 'I'll go upstairs to my room.'

She stormed out.

Teresa had just finished hanging her clothes up, and was preparing to take some away, to iron out the creases.

'I'll do that,' Alex said, speaking Italian.

'Oh, no!' Teresa was shocked. 'You are the mistress.'

'Don't let Rinaldo hear you say that,' Alex muttered. 'Otherwise he may murder me before I murder him.'

She couldn't have explained the annoyance that possessed her. Rinaldo had behaved badly but, with Gino's help, she'd gained the upper hand. The matter should be over.

But it wasn't over while she remembered how he'd set out to take her off guard, and how thoroughly he'd succeeded.

He'd smiled and she'd responded, and in no time at all she'd succumbed to the spell he was weaving. She hadn't even put up a good fight. The moment by the stream, the memories of her mother, even the sunset. He'd known just the right buttons to push, and she'd fallen for it hook, line and sinker.

That must have given him a laugh.

Pushing him firmly out of her head, she took a good look around the room and liked what she saw. It was out of another age, with dark oak furniture and a polished wooden floor. It had none of the modern conveniences of her bedroom at home, expensively designed and tailored to her exact specifications. But she loved it.

There was still some light outside, although it was fading fast. Driven by a sudden impulse, she slipped out of the door, down the stairs and outside.

After the heat of the day the air was blessedly cool and she stood drinking it in.

'Are you still talking to me?'

She turned, laughing, at the sound of Gino's voice.

'You're not the one I'm mad at,' she told him. 'Quite the reverse.'

'That sounds hopeful.'

'I mean that you helped me out. I really like the idea of staying here, but after the way your brother behaved, well—if you hadn't done your going-down-on-one-knee act, I'd have had to leave, simply to make my point.'

'It wasn't an act,' he said at once. 'In my heart I'm always down on one knee to you.'

'Stop your nonsense,' she told him amiably, 'or I'll take you seriously, and then where would you be?'

'In heaven! All right, I take it back if you don't like it. Let me show you the stables. There's a horse there that would just suit you.'

As they started to walk there was the sound of pattering from behind them, and the next moment Brutus wandered out, making for Alex.

'Hey,' she said, fondling his ears and trying to dodge his madly licking tongue. 'All right, don't eat me. All right, all right!'

She nuzzled him, burying her face pleasurably against his soft fur.

'He was Maria's,' Gino said. 'She brought him with her to the wedding, as a puppy. He's very old now, but Rinaldo spends a fortune on keeping him alive and fit. He's got arthritis, but as long as he has expensive injections every month, it's kept at bay. I'll swear he spends more on Brutus than he does on himself.'

Alex remembered how Rinaldo had driven the dog inside when she'd tried to make a fuss of him. She'd put it down to irritation, but now she saw the action in a new light; possessiveness about the only living creature that still reminded him of his wife.

But it had been years. How long could a man mourn?

Gino led her through the trees to where there was a long, low building, with cars parked in one section and horses housed in another.

Switching on the light, he led her into the stables where three animals looked at them curiously.

'That big brute at the end is Rinaldo's,' Gino said, pointing to a fierce-looking horse. 'This one is mine, and this third one is a kind of spare. I think you'd like him.'

He was a chestnut with mild eyes, and Alex did like him.

'We'll go out tomorrow,' Gino said, 'in the late afternoon, when we're back from the funeral, and it's cooler.'

As they left the stable he slipped an arm around her waist and drew her close, managing to drop a light kiss on her mouth.

'Behave yourself,' she said, escaping and running back to the house.

Laughing, he followed her, managing to catch up just by the porch lamp.

'You're a hard-hearted woman,' he complained. 'Or shall I go down on one knee again?'

'Don't be a fool,' she said tenderly. 'And let me go. It's time I was in bed.'

His answer was too tighten his arms and steal another kiss, but he did it with such delicacy that she couldn't be annoyed. He was like a playful puppy who only needed some affection to make him quiet again.

'Alex,' he murmured after a while, 'Couldn't we—?'

'No, we couldn't,' she said firmly. 'Now, that's enough. I'm an engaged woman.'

'But if you weren't, you and I—'

'I said that's enough,' she said, trying not to laugh.

'Just one more kiss.'

He managed to sneak one before she got away and ran indoors. Gino took a deep breath of joy, throwing back his head so that when he opened his eyes he was looking directly at the moon.

'Hm!'

The wry grunt from overhead made him turn and see his brother standing at an open window.

'I suppose you saw everything?' he asked.

'Enough!' Rinaldo growled.

'She loves me. She loves me.'

'Go to bed,' Rinaldo said, shutting his window firmly.

Enrico's funeral was scheduled for the next day at two o'clock in the great Duomo. His Florence relatives had insisted on that location as the only one suitable for a man of his prominence.

During the morning Rinaldo said to Alex, 'I imagine you'll wish to bring your luggage into town so that you can check back into the hotel.'

'Now, why would I want to do that?'

'I gathered you were only too anxious to depart.'

'That was before Gino asked me so nicely to stay. I found his invitation irresistible.'

Her ironic tone left no doubt that this was a challenge. It provoked Rinaldo to say softly, 'Do not play games with me.'

'I'm not playing games. I'm accepting an invitation that you yourself were the first to issue. You do remember that, don't you?'

He glowered without replying, and she sensed that this kind of duelling talk set him at a disadvantage. If he could have simply thrown her into the car he would have done so. As it was, they were now fighting on her terms.

'You know, you might actually regret bringing me here,' she mused, giving him a teasing smile.

'I regret it already,' he growled.

'Is everything all right?' Gino asked, appearing suddenly.

'Everything's fine,' Alex assured him. 'Rinaldo was

just hoping that I'd had a good night, and would want to make a really long stay.'

'And you know that's what I want, too,' Gino said, slipping an arm about her waist. 'Promise that you're going to stay.'

'For as long as you want me,' she assured him.

Rinaldo walked away without another word.

The three of them travelled to Florence. As they entered the Duomo heads turned towards them. She saw Montelli and the chagrined look that crossed his face at the sight of them together.

This was what Rinaldo had meant about keeping the others away. Alex smiled. Now she'd recovered from her annoyance she was almost grateful to him—almost, but not quite—for doing her a service.

At the reception afterwards her lawyer, Isidoro, approached her.

'I've promised a dozen people that you'll talk to them,' he said.

'Of course—later. Much later.'

'But look—'

'I told you, and you can tell them, the Farnese brothers have to have their chance first.'

He dropped his voice.

'I saw them arrive with you, one each side like warders. Are they keeping you prisoner?'

Alex shook her head, her eyes gleaming with mischief.

'Actually,' she said, 'it's the other way around. I've got my own agenda.'

'Do the Farneses know what it is?'

'They think they do. Get rid of the vultures for me Isidoro. Tell them I'll get round to them if and when it suits me.'

She would have escaped right then, but her cousins

descended on her with eager protestations of affection. When Alex rejoined the brothers a few minutes later she was smiling.

'What's so funny?' Rinaldo wanted to know.

'They all invited me to dinner. I said yes, as long as I could bring the two of you.' She chuckled. 'That put them right off.'

A shout of laughter was surprised from Rinaldo.

'We'll go one better and invite them all ourselves,' he suggested.

'I couldn't advise them to accept,' Alex said. 'I don't know what you might put in the soup. Or then again— maybe I do.'

Rinaldo grinned at her. It had a touch of the conspirator.

CHAPTER SIX

GOING down to an early breakfast next morning Rinaldo found his brother standing at the landing window gazing out at something that was enjoying his full attention.

'Any excuse not to start work,' he said.

'Well that is quite some excuse,' Gino said, not taking his eyes from the figure running through the trees.

At first Rinaldo saw only a flash of scarlet. Then it resolved itself into a slim, perfectly honed female body, clad in tight-fitting scarlet shorts that smoothed their way over her hips almost down to her knees, gleaming with every movement she made.

Above a bare midriff she wore a matching scarlet sports bra that left no doubts as to the beauty of her figure.

This was Alex's daily workout, and she was running with great intensity, her eyes fixed just ahead, breathing steadily and powerfully.

The brothers watched as she headed for the barn and went inside. After exchanging puzzled frowns they went downstairs and out in the direction of the barn.

They soon saw what had made her choose this place. Part of the barn was only one storey high, and the ceiling was crossed from side to side with wooden beams. To one of these Alex had attached hanging rings and was swinging along from one to the other hand over hand. A bale of hay just below showed how she had managed to launch herself up there.

Inch by inch she swung along the rings. At the end

she turned and started the journey back, heading for the bale where she could land easily.

But then Gino was there, kicking the bale aside, reaching up to receive her.

'Come on,' he cried.

Alex took a deep breath and launched herself forward, landing in a pair of powerful hands.

But they were Rinaldo's.

Somehow he had taken Gino's place and was now holding her with his hands about her bare midriff, looking up at her with a face full of grim irony.

'Oi!' Gino protested. 'No need to shove me out of the way like that.'

'There was every need,' Rinaldo said. 'We haven't got time for you two to fool around. This is a busy, working farm.'

'But you had no right—'

'Could you two have your private argument some other time?' Alex demanded, incensed. 'I'd like to get down.'

Rinaldo lowered her to the floor. After her exertions she was breathing hard and heat seemed to be pounding through her body.

'Thank you,' she gasped.

'Do you intend to indulge in these antics very often?' he asked politely.

'I exercise every day. It keeps me fit.'

'Working on the farm has the same effect,' he observed drily. 'You might find it interesting. In the meantime, if you intend to go on doing this, may I suggest you dress more modestly? I don't want my workers distracted.'

He walked away without looking back, so he didn't see Alex lunge after him, only restrained by Gino.

'Save it,' he said.

'I'll kill him!' she muttered. 'I'll kill him!'

'Nah! Fantasise about it like the rest of us do.'

'What does he mean *modestly*?'

'Well, you are quite an eyeful, and an armful.'

He wrapped his arms about her waist, making no effort to release her.

'Well, you'd better let me go,' she said grumpily. 'It wouldn't do for me to *distract* you.'

'You distract me all the time,' he said wistfully.

'Gino!' came a yell from outside.

'Let's kill him together,' Gino muttered, releasing her, resignedly.

Before having breakfast Alex took a cool shower. She felt hot all through, deep down, intensely hot in a way that no water could soothe. The feeling had been there since Rinaldo's hands had encircled her waist, holding her against him.

Perhaps it was lucky, she thought, that Gino had not caught her. He would certainly have turned that intimate moment into a kiss.

But Rinaldo had been completely unmoved.

She rubbed soap over the place, feeling again the pressure of his fingers, and the warmth going through her in endless waves. She turned the water onto cold, and let it lave her again and again, hoping for the feeling to go.

She waited a long time before going downstairs, and when she did she found that the brothers had gone.

Despite the occasional battles Alex found her introduction to Belluna genuinely fascinating. Rinaldo had given her a view from a distance, but now she rode with Gino, getting a closer view of fields full of corn and olives, vineyards stretching away on steep slopes.

'We grow the Sangiovese grapes that make Chianti,' he said. '*True* Chianti, made and bottled in this region. We have our imitators all over the world, but they're not the same.'

His voice contained a hint of Tuscan arrogance, that made Alex smile, realising that there was more to him than an easygoing charmer.

But for pure arrogance, the kind that made her want to dance with rage, she thought there was no beating Rinaldo. He made no comment about their long absences together. The whole matter seemed beneath his notice. Nor did he show much interest when they discussed their adventures in the evening.

He would listen, grunting, to the day's events, then take himself off to his study at the first opportunity.

'He makes me want to bang my head against the wall,' Alex raged one evening when he'd gone.

'Bang *his*,' Gino suggested. 'More fun.'

'Ah, but would I make any impression on it?'

'Not a hope. People have been trying for years.'

'How does anyone put up with him?' Alex asked bitterly. There was something about the way Rinaldo overlooked her that made her seethe.

'It takes long practise,' Gino said, yawning. 'It's been a tiring day.'

'Yes, I'm going straight to bed.'

She had grown even more fond of the bedroom, whose décor and furniture were so far behind the times. She had soon gotten into the Italian habit of stripping off the duvet and all the sheets each morning and hanging them out of the window to air. Teresa protested that a guest should not be working, but Alex enjoyed the job.

She particularly relished the moment when she'd lost her grip, and the duvet fell from the window, landing on

Rinaldo who happened to be underneath. His yell and the infuriated look he cast up at her were among her happiest memories. In fact, much the pleasure of her stay lay in the knowledge that she was infuriating him.

'Teresa is upset with you,' he observed one morning at breakfast.

'Yes, I know. She thinks it's shocking that I do my own room and help her in the kitchen.'

'Then why hurt her feelings?'

'Because I don't want to put any more burdens onto her aching bones. Have either of you any idea how old Teresa is?'

'Older than I can count, I know that,' Gino said.

'Do you really think she can manage this great house with no help?'

'I've offered to get someone else in,' Rinaldo informed her. 'She won't have it.'

Alex made a sound of exasperation intended to cover all men.

'And you left matters there because it was convenient,' she snorted. 'Great!'

'May I remind you that my father was alive until recently?' Rinaldo said coldly. 'It was his decision.'

'Then it was the wrong decision and you should have overruled him. Don't tell me you couldn't have done that. Teresa is an old woman and it's too much for her. She won't admit it because she's proud, and she's afraid you'll send her away.'

'What nonsense! Of course I wouldn't!'

'Don't tell me, tell her. Say she's got to have someone else in to do the heavy work, whether she likes it or not. Be firm. Are you a man or a mouse?'

'I'm beginning to wonder,' he said, eyeing her grimly.

'Oh, stop that! You know I'm right.'

'Heaven preserve me from women who say, "You know I'm right".'

'Yes, because you know they are.'

'Can't you two talk without fighting?' Gino asked plaintively.

Alex shrugged. 'It's as good a way of communicating as any other,' she said, her eyes on Rinaldo. 'At least it's honest. People are never so sincere as when they're abusing each other.'

'I don't understand that,' Gino said.

But Rinaldo understood perfectly. She could see that. He was giving her the same look of ironic complicity that she'd seen after Enrico's funeral. It said that they saw the world through the same eyes, and to hell with the others.

'I'm merely astonished at your extravagance,' he said. 'The more wages I have to pay the longer you have to wait for your money.'

Alex rolled her eyes to heaven.

'Give me patience!' she implored some unseen deity. 'This house is full of empty rooms. The new maid will live in one of them, which will be part of her wages that will cost you nothing. You see? All problems solved.'

'When I consider how anxious I was to bring you here,' Rinaldo observed, 'I can only wonder at my own foolishness.'

'For pity's sake stop arguing,' she told him. 'Just do it. Soften it by telling Teresa she can choose the person herself. She's probably got a relative who'd be ideal. Go on. Do it.'

'You're taking a risk,' Gino muttered, his eyes on his brother as if he was a lion about to spring. 'He doesn't like being ordered about. Never fear. I'll protect you.'

'I can protect myself against Rinaldo perfectly, thank

you,' Alex said, although she too was watching him carefully. 'After all, what can he do to me?'

'Throw you out,' Rinaldo growled.

'Not you,' she jeered. 'You might think you want to, but then you wouldn't have me under your eye. Think of the sleep you'd lose, wondering what I was doing, who I was seeing. No, I'm safe enough.'

'Alex,' Gino begged, 'please be careful.'

'Who wants to be careful? That's boring.' She was enjoying herself.

'I understood,' Rinaldo said frostily, 'that we were to have first refusal.'

'Certainly. That's what I'll tell Montelli and all the others, but who's to say I can't tell them over a candlelit supper?'

'Hey,' Gino said at once, 'if there are any candlelit suppers to be bought, I'll buy them.'

'With champagne?'

'With anything you want, *amor mio*.'

Rinaldo rose sharply and went into the kitchen. A little later they heard the sound of argument and weeping, interspersed with Rinaldo's voice, speaking more gently than Alex had ever heard before.

The next day he drove Teresa to the village where she had been born, about fifty miles away. When they returned in the evening they were accompanied by two hefty young women whom Teresa introduced as her great-nieces, Celia and Franca.

When she had shepherded them into the house Rinaldo detained Alex with a touch on her arm.

'Thank you,' he said gruffly. 'I never thought of it but—you were right.'

Alex smiled. 'She'll be happier with their company, too.'

'I never thought of that either. She and Poppa used to chat in the evenings sometimes, when he wasn't out with Enrico. Since he died she sits in the kitchen alone. Why did you see it and not me?'

'I'm a stranger. Our eyes always see the most clearly.'

'You are no stranger,' he said abruptly, and walked away.

Within a couple of days Celia and Franca had brought the heavy work under their expert control, leaving only the cooking to Teresa. This she guarded jealously.

Whether Rinaldo had told her or whether she had guessed the truth Alex couldn't say. But it was clear that she now regarded Alex as a friend. She would take special care in serving her food, and her eyes would meet hers in a silent question. *Was this how she liked it? Yes? Bene!*

On those occasions Alex would look up to find Rinaldo regarding her, and remember the odd note in his voice when he said, 'You are no stranger.'

She rented another car and, with the knowledge that she now had independence of movement, she no longer felt any need to leave the farm.

Evenings that had once been spent going to parties and first nights were now spent contentedly combing grass seeds out of Brutus's long fur. He came to expect it and would present himself, rolling over on his back to make it easy.

'I used to do that,' Rinaldo observed, 'but these days he tends to stay in the house, so he doesn't wander among the long grass so much, and it stopped being necessary. Until now.'

'He joins me when I run in the morning,' she said. 'At least, he starts out with me, then drops out when he gets tired, and goes and waits for me in the barn. When I swing from the rings he watches in a puzzled sort of way, and you can almost hear him thinking, 'What on earth is she *doing*?'

'We're the best of friends now, aren't we, old boy?' she asked Brutus tenderly. 'And if I don't get these seeds out, you're going to grow a lawn.'

Rinaldo no longer seemed to object to her petting Brutus, and when she looked up a moment later she found him looking at her with a faint smile on his face.

One day he said to her, 'It would be doing me a favour if you'd wait in the house this morning. The vet is coming to give Brutus his injection, and if I'm not back in time at least you'll be with him.'

'Of course. The vet comes all the way out here?'

'You mean, why don't I take Brutus to the surgery? Because he hates cars and goes mad in them, climbing all over the place. That's bad for his arthritis.' After a moment he added uneasily, 'Of course, it costs a lot more—'

'So I'll have to wait an extra five minutes for the money? I wish you'd stop saying things like that.'

'I'm merely trying to assure you that I'm not being wilfully extravagant—'

'No, you're not,' she said indignantly. 'You're rubbing my nose in it. It's worth the expenditure to save Brutus pain, *and you knew I'd say that, so please let it drop*.'

He nodded, and left.

She spent the morning sitting on the sofa with the old dog, who panted in a way she hadn't seen before and was disinclined to move.

At last the vet arrived. He was a youngish man called Silvio, whom Alex liked at once. She explained who she was but had the feeling he already knew. Was there anyone in the whole of Tuscany who didn't know the situation, she wondered?

'How long has he been panting like this?' he asked when he saw Brutus.

'Since this morning. I thought his arthritis must be hurting since it must be so long since his last injection. But the next one will make it all right, won't it?'

'I can take away that pain, but this is something else.' Silvio felt in Brutus's throat, and the dog whined softly. 'There's a lump there, and at his age it's probably bad news. Look at how white his snout is. He's very old. He's had his life. The kindest thing now is to let him go peacefully.'

'I can't authorise you to do that,' Alex said. 'He's Rinaldo's dog.'

'Tell him to call me and I'll come back, preferably today. Rinaldo can't put the inevitable off any longer. Do you still want me to give him the injection?'

'Of course,' she said at once.

When Silvio had gone Alex rubbed the dog's head, laid trustingly in her lap.

'How is he ever going to let you go?' she murmured. 'You were *her* dog. You're all he has of her.'

Gino returned first. When she told him what had happened he dropped to his knees beside Brutus, patting him and murmuring sympathetically.

Rinaldo arrived a few minutes later and Brutus slid off the sofa and went to meet him. He was moving more easily now, and Alex watched the pleasure come into Rinaldo's face as he saw the improvement and ran his hands over the rough coat.

'Thank you,' he told Alex. 'He's still panting a bit though. Did the vet have anything to say about that?'

'Yes, he thinks it's something bad,' Alex said. 'He

wants you to call him and discuss—' she hesitated '—putting him to sleep.'

'Nonsense,' Rinaldo said impatiently. 'A good meal is all he needs.'

'I fed him this afternoon. He only ate a little and then he brought it up.'

'He'll eat what *I* give him. You'll see.'

But Brutus only stared mournfully at the food his master put down for him.

'Come on,' Rinaldo urged gently. 'It's your favourite.'

The dog looked up at him with eyes that Alex couldn't bear to see. They were full of understanding, and trust that his master would face the truth and do what must be done.

Rinaldo saw Alex and Gino looking at him.

'You'd think no dog had ever been off his food before,' he snapped.

He went into the next room and they heard him on the phone to Silvio. When he came back he said,

'He's on his way. I'm going for a walk.'

He didn't speak to Brutus but he looked at him, and the old dog wandered slowly out after his master, into the twilight.

Gino sighed. 'He hasn't seen it yet.'

'He's seen it,' Alex said softly.

Silvio arrived in an hour to find Rinaldo and Brutus sitting under the trees. Gino and Alex went out and arrived as the vet was saying, 'All I can do is give him some tablets, that would keep him with you for a few more weeks. But they wouldn't be happy weeks. Not for him.'

Rinaldo shrugged. 'That settles it. The barn is the best place.'

He began to walk away, Brutus following.

'Shall we come?' Gino asked.

'No need,' Rinaldo said over his shoulder.

Silvio followed them into the barn and remained for ten minutes before coming out and driving away.

After a moment Rinaldo emerged. His manner was calm and his face betrayed nothing. He shut the barn and walked off under the trees.

Alex spent the rest of that evening alone with Gino, talking in a half-hearted fashion.

Rinaldo returned after an hour, brushed aside their attempts at conversation and went straight to his office, where Teresa brought him coffee.

Gino, who made a well-intentioned visit, returned looking glum.

'Rinaldo says he has to concentrate on the books. He says there's work to be done and he can't waste time on something that's finished with. When I left he was studying figures.'

'The ultimate sign of heartlessness, according to him,' Alex said wryly.

'Heartless is right,' Gino snapped.

Rinaldo had not appeared when Alex went to bed. She tried to sleep but couldn't, and at last she got up and went to stand at the window, where a full moon was turning the land to silver.

Suddenly she grew still. From down below she could see movement, as though someone was hiding just beyond the trees.

Pulling on her dressing gown she left her room and went along the corridor to Rinaldo's room. But her knock produced no response. After a moment she knocked louder, but still there was no answer.

She stood in the hallway, listening to the quiet of the

house about her, unwilling to try again and awake Rinaldo for what might be nothing. She could imagine his caustic remarks.

After a moment she turned away and went down the stairs, into the corridor that led to the back door. She could just make out that that there was still someone beyond the trees. Now she could also hear the sound of rhythmic movement.

She stepped forward as silently as possible, gliding through the trees until she came to a small clearing. Then she stopped. What she saw made her draw a sharp breath and step back quickly.

The man in the clearing would not want anyone to see what he was doing, and especially he would not want to be seen by her.

The spade flashed as the hole grew deeper. Rinaldo stood inside, waist deep. He wore no shirt and his body gleamed with perspiration as it rose and fell. His concentration was fierce and total.

At last he stopped, leaning on the spade, his head bent, his shoulders heaving. Then he straightened up, and reached out to something Alex had not noticed before.

Now she saw that Brutus was lying on the ground. She waited for Rinaldo to toss him into the grave, but instead he drew the cold body toward him and gathered it into his arms. Slowly he began to lower it.

Alex held her breath, awed by his incredible gentleness to an animal who could no longer feel it.

At the last moment he paused and laid his cheek against Brutus's head. For a long time he was still. Then he moved his head slightly, caressing the fur, and she thought she saw something shining on his cheek. Still he held his friend, as though unable to face the final moment.

'Perdona mi! Ti prego perdona mi!'

Forgive me. Please forgive me. The last words she had ever expected to hear from this unrelenting man.

At last he dropped to his knees, out of Alex's sight. He remained there for a long time.

She backed away slowly, knowing that he must not find her here. When she was safely out of the trees she began to run back to the house. As she went, she called herself a fool.

She had never known anything about Rinaldo. Or rather, she had known exactly what he wanted her to know, and no more. Tonight she had witnessed a consuming grief that he would keep hidden from the world, if he could.

Nobody saw her slip into the house, for which she was thankful. She wouldn't have known what to say to Gino just now.

Once in her room she went to the window and waited. At last, after a long time, he emerged from the trees. She stepped back from the window, lest he see her, but he walked with his head down and his shoulders hunched, not looking about him. As she watched, he crossed the yard and disappeared.

At breakfast next morning Rinaldo looked as though he hadn't slept. Which was probably true, Alex thought. His face was pale beneath his tan, and she could see the tension about his mouth

She longed to say something that would ease his pain, but she knew he would never let her get so close, and would resent her for even trying.

He didn't sit down, but snatched up a coffee in one hand and a roll in the other, eating on his feet as though longing to be gone.

Gino came into the kitchen, looking worried.

'I've just been to the barn. Brutus has gone.'

Rinaldo shrugged. 'So?'

'I thought we might bury him properly.'

'What for?' Rinaldo asked coldly.

'What for? You loved him. I did too, but you and he were so close—'

'He was a dog, Gino. Dogs come and go.'

'But—'

'I've already disposed of him.'

'*Disposed* of him?' Gino echoed, aghast. 'Like a piece of rubbish? That was Brutus! How can you be so callous?'

'He was dead,' Rinaldo said, his voice on the edge of exasperation. 'There was nothing more to say or do. He was dead.'

'So you just threw him out. No grave, no—'

'I advise you to grow up and stop being sentimental,' Rinaldo said coldly.

He drained his cup and walked out quickly before his brother could speak again.

'Well, I'll be—!' Gino almost tore his hair. 'He was supposed to love that dog. Some kind of love!'

'People have their own way of showing their feelings,' Alex suggested.

'Always supposing that they have any feelings. Brutus is dead. Chuck him out! That's how Rinaldo sees it. He didn't even cry when the poor old fellow died.'

'You don't know. We weren't there.'

'You saw his face when he came out of the barn. Blank.'

'But that doesn't mean anything,' Alex protested, thinking about the tell-tale gleam she'd seen the night before, as Rinaldo laid his face against the lifeless dog.

'He wouldn't let anyone see. He'd probably think it was weakness.'

'Rinaldo thinks *having* feelings is weakness, never mind showing them. That's why he cuts them right out.'

For the first time she found herself irritated by Gino.

'I'll bet you don't know half as much as you think you do,' she said. 'Maybe a stranger can pick up more—'

'Oh ho! Here comes woman's intuition!'

'Here comes the coffee to pour over your head if you talk like that.'

He grinned and hopped nimbly out of the way.

'Pax! I take it back. But trust me on this. I understand Rinaldo as you never will.'

And I, she thought, am beginning to understand him in way that nobody else does.

She didn't know what else to say. She longed to make Gino see the truth about his brother, but it was Rinaldo's secret and she had no right to betray it.

CHAPTER SEVEN

FRUSTRATED, she went out into the yard. A movement from the barn drew her steps there, and she found Rinaldo.

'Have you come to tell me what a heartless monster I am, too?' he asked ironically. 'Because if so, don't.'

'No, I won't say that. After last night, I know better.'

He shot her a sharp glance. 'What do you mean?'

'I saw you bury Brutus.'

For a moment he was quite still. Then he said curtly, 'Nonsense.'

'It isn't. I noticed something moving in the trees and went down. I was there while you dug the grave and put him in it. I saw—everything.'

'You have a vivid imagination, I'll say that for you. You and Gino make a good pair.'

Anger at his rebuff made her snap, 'You think Gino would be interested in what I saw? Let's try.'

She turned to go but he was beside her in a flash, seizing her arms in a fierce grip.

'Don't dare to tell him anything,' he growled. 'What concern is it of yours what I do?'

'But it's true, isn't it? Losing him broke your heart. Why deny it?'

'Because it's nobody else's business!'

'But he's your brother. Don't you think he'd feel for you?'

'I don't ask him to feel for me. Nor do I ask you.'

'Who do you ask?' she said quietly. 'Now Brutus is dead, who do you share your feelings with?'

'There's a lot to be said for a dog,' he snapped. 'They keep quiet and they don't fret about things that are none of their business. Why did you have to come Belluna and interfere?'

'You more or less forced me to come.'

'And it was the worst day's work I ever did.'

'You said I needed to learn about this place and the things that went on in it. That's just what I'm doing. I'm learning that nothing is ever quite what it seems.'

'What does that mean?'

'You, for instance. You work hard at being one thing and seeming another. I wonder why.'

'It keeps me safe from snoopers.'

'Does that include Gino? Because you hide from him too. You don't let anyone in, do you? Except Brutus.'

His fingers tightened on her shoulders, giving her a tiny shake.

'Will you stop?' he asked fiercely. *'Will you stop?'*

'I'm sorry,' she said gently after a moment. 'I know it isn't really my business. But now I can't help getting involved. Where do I draw the line?'

'Right here,' he said, still holding her. 'You've reached the boundary. Stay on your side of it, and we'll manage.'

Suddenly she realised that he was shaking. Through the contact of his fingers on her bare arms she could sense his whole body vibrating.

In her turn she reached up to take hold of his arms.

'Rinaldo,' she said. 'Don't shut me out. Let me help.'

'I don't need your help.'

But she refused to be snubbed. 'After last night it's too late,' she said quietly. 'I know what I know.'

She knew she was treading on dangerous ground and

for a moment she thought he would lose his temper. But instead he sighed and the anger went out of his face.

'How can *you* possibly help?' he asked heavily.

'You mean I'm the last person who ever could. Because I caused all the trouble, didn't I?'

Hearing his own accusation put so bluntly seemed to do something to Rinaldo. She saw his eyes full of shock as he realised that he was still holding her. He dropped his hands from her arms.

There was an ache inside her that had something to do with his misery. She wanted to assuage it and ease the hurt for them both.

He sat down on a bale of hay, leaning back against a post of the barn, his hands hanging loose as though he'd lost the will to fight.

'No, it's not your fault,' he said tiredly. 'I know I said that at first, but in truth I know better. It wasn't you who created the situation.'

He took a long breath. His face was livid.

'It was my father,' he said at last. 'A man I trusted, and who let me live in a fool's paradise. He never warned me, that's what—' He made a confused gesture.

'That's what hurts, isn't it?' she whispered, sitting beside him.

His eyes were full of resignation, almost despair.

'Yes,' he said simply. 'We used to sit up late at night, discussing problems. I thought we were a team, and all the time he was keeping me at a distance, not trusting me with the truth.'

'Oh, no,' she said at once. 'It wasn't like that.'

'How can you possibly know?'

'Because in an odd way I feel as if I do know him. Everyone talks about how lovely he was, laughing, singing, always looking on the bright side. I think that probably made him a wonderful person and a loveable father, but maybe not a very practical farmer.'

He nodded. 'That's true.'

'But you *are* practical. I expect you hauled him back from the brink a few times.'

'That's true as well. He was always going after madcap schemes and having to be rescued. You'd think he'd learn.'

Alex shook her head.

'People like that never do learn,' she said gently. 'They're always sure they're going to get it right next time. I think he relied on you completely, and was just a little bit in awe of you.'

'Nonsense, how could my father—?' But Rinaldo checked himself, and a strange, distant look came over his face, as though he were hearing distant echoes.

'Perhaps,' he said after a while.

'You've said that the money helped this place.'

'A lot. Poppa ploughed it into Belluna—he was a good enough farmer for that. The investment has enabled us to prosper as never before.'

'Then don't you see how he must have cherished his secret, the feeling that *he'd* done something to make things right, instead of leaving it all to you? He probably looked forward to surprising you with it one day, rather like a child springing a surprise on an adult and saying, "There, aren't I clever? What do you think of *that*?"'

Rinaldo stared at her, as if thunderstruck.

'Yes,' he murmured. 'That's exactly how he was. I can hear how he would have said it.'

'It isn't his fault that it all went wrong,' she pleaded. 'He couldn't have known what would happen. Maybe it hurt his pride to have to depend on you so much. He wanted you to admire him.'

'You make it sound so convincing,' he said in a low voice. 'If only I could remember—'

'Remember what?'

'Something—anything—just a moment that would tell me what was in his mind. I keep having this feeling that it's there, just on the edge. Like when you see something out of the corner of your eye, but when you turn it vanishes. I dream about it, but it isn't there when I awaken. Maybe it doesn't really exist at all.'

'If it does, it will come back to you,' she said. 'Not now, because your head's all scrambled, but when you feel easier inside.'

His mouth quirked wryly.

'I think I've forgotten what it's like to feel easy inside.'

She looked at his hands, lying loosely clasped. He was a big man and his hands were large in proportion. She could still feel their power where he'd gripped her. Yet now they looked helpless.

'You carry all the burdens for everyone, don't you?' she said.

He didn't answer, and she wondered if she'd taken a risk too far. But his eyes held only a searching look, as though he were trying to fathom her.

From outside came Gino's voice.

'Hey! Anybody there?'

He was coming toward the barn. Rinaldo put his finger to his lips, shaking his head slightly, and hurried out before Gino could enter.

She heard his voice carrying back.

'I was just coming. We have a lot to do today.'

Their voices faded. After a while she slipped out of the barn to find everywhere quiet.

She went indoors and put through a call to David, but there was only his answerphone. They had spoken several times since she came to Belluna. She had apologised for being so long, and he'd encouraged her to stay as long as necessary.

She always finished these calls feeling a little guilty that he was being so nice and understanding. She felt she was taking advantage of his patience to indulge herself.

One thing she was sure of. There was no way she was leaving before the Feast of St Romauld, which took place on June 19th.

'There's a parade of floats through the streets,' Gino told her, 'and we all wander around eating and drinking, and then we dance. I shall dance only with you, *amor mio*. And you must dance only with me.'

'She can't do that,' Rinaldo said at once. 'Montelli and the others will want some of her attention, and you must do what's necessary to keep them dangling, eh, Alex?' He spoke pleasantly, as though this were an accepted joke between them.

'Of course,' she said, playing up to him.

Gino assumed an air of theatrical comedy.

'But why should you need the others when you have us?' he demanded, clasping her waist and leaning over her dramatically.

'Let's say I like some variety,' she chuckled, clinging to him to avoid falling. 'Now, get off me, you great clown.'

When the day arrived, every worker on the farm went to the festival. Families piled into cars, converging on the road to the city so that they ended up in what Gino told her was the Belluna procession.

Alex spent more time choosing what to wear for the festival than she had meant to. Her first choice had been a white dress. But somehow, at the last minute, it seemed wrong.

After trying on one dress after another she came to one of brilliant scarlet that seemed just right. It had a steep V-neck and looked splendid against her light tan.

That was something new. In London she strove to look elegant, businesslike. But not splendid. Suddenly only splendid would do.

One of the hands, who had no family, drove Teresa, Celia and Franca in Rinaldo's old vehicle, while the brothers and Alex went in her shiny hired car.

As they were leaving the house Alex handed her keys to Rinaldo. 'I'm sure you'd rather have these.'

'Be careful Alex,' he said. 'Someone will mistake you for a traditional female, asking a man to drive your car.'

'Nobody who knows me would ever make that mistake,' she said firmly. 'But I can't get used to the steering wheel being on the left when I'm used to the right.'

'Ah, yes, the English drive on the wrong side of the road,' he murmured.

She ignored this flagrant provocation, and said, 'It's probably safer if you drive.'

'I don't believe I heard you say that.'

'Oh, get in and drive,' she said in exasperation.

He grinned and did so. Gino swiftly urged Alex into the back seat, and so the three of them made their way into the city.

The two men were also dressed 'for best' in snowy white shirts with ruffled fronts. Gino was by nature a stylish dresser, but, except for the funerals Alex had not seen Rinaldo in anything but shabby working clothes.

Though alike in features the brothers were different in the impression they made, Gino the more conventionally attractive, Rinaldo the more virile and uncompromising.

It was as well, she thought, that she was 'spoken for',

or these two might have seriously disturbed her equi-librium.

As it was, she was looking forward to spending time at the festival in the company of her two handsome es-corts.

It was late afternoon and things were already happen-ing. Alex found it was nothing like the pallid festivities she'd seen at home.

Figures pranced around the streets. They were all out-rageously clad, some from history, some from mythol-ogy. Saints mingled with demons, sorcerers and clowns.

Several times Alex was seized around the waist and whirled into an impromptu dance, from which Gino had to rescue her.

Rinaldo left them almost as soon as they arrived, but after a while they came across him, deep on conversation with a grave-looking man.

'Bank manager,' Gino muttered.

'In the middle of a festival?' Alex demanded.

'You'd think he could take five minutes off, wouldn't you?'

'Perhaps he's arranging a mortgage on the rest of the property so that he can buy me out quickly.'

'*What?*' Gino was aghast.

'Well, it would solve a lot of problems,' she said, try-ing to sound cheerful.

'No it wouldn't. You'd go away. I don't want you to go. You don't want to go, do you?'

She didn't answer. She couldn't.

The Loggia of the Boar was filled with stalls selling all manner of foods. Gino bought cakes and wine and they wandered around, hand in hand, like children.

As the natural light faded the coloured lights became

brighter. Tables were set out in the streets and a band began to play.

They strolled about until they found Rinaldo, clearly having finished with the bank manager, sitting alone at a table in the Piazza della Signoria, brooding over a solitary glass of wine.

'Hello brother,' Gino cried. 'Are you having a good time? You don't look it.'

'We don't all have to go crazy to enjoy ourselves,' Rinaldo observed, unruffled, as they joined him at the table. 'The procession should be starting about now.'

Even as he spoke trumpets sounded in the distance, and a cheer went up from the crowd as the first floats appeared. Alex watched eagerly.

Although it was a religious festival not all the floats had that theme. Some were so bawdy as to be almost obscene, some were cruel.

Alex stared as one went by depicting a huge figure with a goat's head and flashing eyes. She knew enough symbolism to recognise that the goat represented not only the devil but also human sexuality at its most rampant and uncontrolled.

Yet in the saint's parade he did not seem out of place. Everything here had a red-blooded gusto that thrilled her.

'Some of those floats are amazing,' she mused. 'That one with the baker and the loaf of bread, is it really as rude as it looks?'

'Oh, yes,' Gino said with relish. 'The ruder the better. That's how we like it. That's really why we celebrate St Romauld at all, because he's a great excuse for rudeness.'

'I've never heard of him,' Alex said.

'He's not one of the better known saints,' Rinaldo agreed, 'but he has the advantage of having been thoroughly licentious before he became saintly. He lived about a thousand years ago, and to start with he did a lot of drinking and wenching. Then he reformed and became a monk, founding a monastery not far from here.'

'But he was constantly plagued by temptation.' Gino took up the tale. 'Naturally he resisted it, but it means that his parade can be very colourful. For every one float depicting him as a saint there are about ten showing worldly indulgence. Which is about right,' he added judiciously.

Looking at the floats Alex saw that this was true. The world and the devil were depicted with great imagination, again and again.

'But isn't it supposed to be a religious festival?' she laughed.

'Of course,' Gino said. 'People go to church and say sorry afterwards. But the pleasures of the flesh must come first, and you must really exert yourself to enjoy them, because otherwise the repentance wouldn't be real, and that would be sacrilege.'

Alex poked him in the ribs. 'That sounds a very convenient philosophy.'

'Poppa taught it to me. He said it was ancient tradition, but I think he invented it.'

Rinaldo nodded. 'That wouldn't surprise me.'

Suddenly Alex burst out laughing. 'What on earth is that meant to be?' she asked, pointing at a float that had just come into view.

Seated on it was a very beautiful young woman, with flower-wreathed golden hair that streamed down over her throne. Behind that throne stood a man dressed in gorgeous armour, clearly a victorious warrior.

There were two other men, crouching at the woman's feet. One of them clutched a piglet that squealed and made constant efforts to escape.

As the float rumbled by the piglet managed to free itself, dashed to the edge of the float and took a flying leap. Alex bounded forward just in time to catch it.

'Come on,' she laughed. 'The road's hard. You don't want to land on it.'

She handed it back to the men on the float who cheered her, crying, *'Grazie, Circe!'*

'What did he mean?' she asked, returning to her seat.

'He called you Circe,' Rinaldo told her. 'That woman on the float is meant to be Circe the witch-goddess. She lured men into her cave and turned them into swine.'

'Hence the piglet?' she guessed.

'Yes, he must have been the best they could manage.'

'She wasn't just a witch,' Gino objected. 'She was a healer too. The legend says she was an expert in herbs and potions, and a woman of wisdom. The man standing behind her was the hero Odysseus, who overcame her with love.'

'Did he?' Rinaldo demanded. 'He thought he had, but she was an enchantress who could blind men to everything else. He was on an important journey, but he forgot it and stayed with her for a year. So who overcame who?'

'You don't like her, do you?' Alex challenged him, laughing. 'Fancy a woman getting him to put her first! Shocking! Rinaldo, this is festival. Lighten up for pity's sake.'

Suddenly there was a cry of, *'Gino, hey Gino!'* and three scantily clad young women descended on them, laughing, kissing him, then carrying him off by main force.

He looked back at the other two, giving a shrug of comical, helpless dismay.

'My brother is very popular,' Rinaldo observed. 'But he is more pursued than pursuing.'

'You don't have to excuse him to me,' Alex said cheerfully. 'I'm glad of the chance to sit quietly for a bit.'

'Let me order you some wine.'

'Not wine, thank you.'

'Mineral water?'

'What I'd really love most of all at this moment,' she said wistfully, 'is a nice cup of tea.'

Rinaldo made an imperious gesture to a passing waiter, spoke a few words of Tuscan and handed over a note. The waiter nodded and scurried away.

'I don't believe it,' Alex said admiringly. 'You haven't managed to summon up tea in the middle of a wine-drenched festival?'

'We'll have to wait and see.'

In a few minutes the tea arrived and she sipped it in ecstasy.

'Nothing ever tasted as good as this,' she sighed. 'Thank you.'

Then her eyes widened in horror.

'Oh, goodness, look! Over there. Montelli. He's been following me around.'

'Shall I leave you free to talk to him?'

Rinaldo made to rise but Alex stopped him with a hand on his arm.

'Don't you dare. I rely on you to get rid of him for me.'

'Thus confirming my poor reputation. Do you know that I'm commonly held to have taken you prisoner and kept you apart from the world?'

'Well, that was the original idea, wasn't it?' she teased.

'I really can't remember,' he said self-consciously.

Montelli reached them, beaming in a way that didn't

hide his anxiety. He would have taken Gino's seat but
Alex dumped her bag on it too quickly for him.

'*Signorina*, what a pleasure! It's so hard to reach you
these days.'

'Yes, I'm afraid I keep my phone turned off,' she said.
'You must blame this lovely country which is taking all
my attention.'

'Indeed, Italy is ideal for a vacation, but perhaps a fair-
skinned northerner shouldn't live here permanently.'

'How kind of you to be concerned for my welfare!'
Alex said, with a dazzling smile. 'Would it really trouble
you if I decided to stay?'

At this hint that she might not sell at all, Montelli paled
visibly.

'Well of course we should all be delighted—good
heavens, you're drinking tea. Is this fellow too mean to
buy you a proper glass of wine?'

'Far too mean,' Rinaldo said in a voice that suggested
he might be enjoying himself.

'How shocking. *Signorina*, let me take you somewhere
and buy you champagne.'

His hand clutched her arm determinedly. The next moment his yell split the air and he was frantically dabbing
hot tea from his trousers.

'I'm so sorry,' Alex exclaimed unconvincingly. 'I
can't think how it happened.'

He gave her a look of wild accusation but was too
wise to speak, and scuttled away.

'Why didn't you come to my rescue?' she demanded
of Rinaldo.

'I never saw a woman less in need of rescue,' he said,
with a grin. '*I* could hardly have thrown tea over him.'

'It was an accident.'

'Of course. I've had a few such accidents myself.'

'I'll bet you have!'

Now the procession had finished and the streets were full of revellers. Somewhere in the distance they could see Gino, flowers in his hair, dancing with three partners at once.

'What does he think he's doing?' Rinaldo demanded.

Alex chuckled. 'I think he's making sure that he won't commit sacrilege the next time he goes to church.'

'Shall I fetch him for you?'

'What for? He's a free agent.'

'And you? Are you free? With a fiancé in England?'

'Yes,' she said hastily, struggling to remember David's face. 'I meant that—Gino—'

'Gino and you spend a lot of time together.'

'Only because you put him up to it,' she retorted with spirit. 'Leave him alone. Let him enjoy himself.'

A dancing couple nearly crashed into their table.

'If you've finished your tea, perhaps we should move,' Rinaldo said. 'It isn't very safe here.'

She followed him out of the piazza and down side streets until they reached the river, where a blessedly cool breeze was blowing. He took her arm to steer her to the water's side, and they stood there for a moment enjoying the night air.

Looking down into the waters of the Arno, Alex wondered at the change in herself. Her light tan made her dark blue eyes seem larger. She could see that much in the ghostly figure who looked back at her from the dark water.

No, she thought. Not so much a ghost as an echo of another self that she might have been. Perhaps still might.

'What are you thinking?' Rinaldo asked suddenly.

'About myself,' she said, still looking down into the water. 'Wondering who I am.'

'I too have wondered that. You are not the person I thought at first.'

'Nobody could be that woman,' Alex said, looking at him with a faint smile. 'She came out of a horror story.'

He nodded. 'I never thanked you.'

'For what?'

'Looking after Brutus. Seeing things about him that I ought to have seen. I let him live too long. I should have done it weeks ago, but I blinded myself to the signs because I couldn't bear to part with him.'

'Was that why you asked him to forgive you?'

'Yes,' he said in a low voice.

'He was your wife's dog, wasn't he?'

'I suppose Gino told you.' His lips curved in a tender, reminiscent smile. 'Maria came to our wedding clutching this ridiculous puppy, and she held onto him all through the service because if she put him down he wandered off, and if she handed him to someone else he cried. She said he was the start of our family, that we would have many children and many dogs. But it didn't happen that way.'

He did not add that now he had nothing left of his wife, but Alex sensed that he did not need to. One by one, those he cared for had been taken away from him. Only Gino was left, and despite the brothers' affection she sensed a distance between them, born of the fact that they were opposites.

'You must be so lonely,' she said impulsively, reaching out to touch him.

He looked at her, then at the place where her hand lay on his arm. For a moment she thought he would put his own hand over it, but then a smile came over his face. And when she saw it she knew she had blundered.

It was as implacable as an iron door slammed in her face.

'Not at all,' he said cheerfully, moving his arm away from her. 'Not at all.'

She cursed her own stupidity for going one step too far with this awkward man. At the last moment he had flinched away from her sympathy, as she should have known he would, retreating into mistrust.

Through the silence she was intensely aware of the unease that swept him as he recalled everything he had confided to her, the way he'd lowered his guard, forgetting that she still represented danger.

She thought vainly for something she could say to bring his mind and heart back to her, but it was too late. He had turned and was heading away from her, along the narrow street.

'Let's go and find Gino,' he called back over his shoulder.

CHAPTER EIGHT

'NEVER mind Gino,' she said desperately. 'I don't own him, and he'd be the first to say so.'

'Is that why I see the two of you fooling around together all the time?' He spoke ironically, and there was a touch of the old edge in his voice as he added, 'I wonder what you'll tell your fiancé.'

'I shan't mention it at all. There's no need.'

'What a very cool race the English must be. If you were my woman I'd want to know that you'd been flirting with another man.'

If I were your woman I wouldn't be flirting with another man.

The thought flashed across her mind before she could stop it. Then it was gone, whispering away into the shadows.

'I wonder if you really would want to know,' she said.

'Yes, because then I could do something about it.'

She understood his meaning perfectly. She should stop him here. But she didn't want to.

'I doubt if you could,' she dared him.

The next moment his arm was across her chest, preventing her going any further, urging her gently but firmly back against the wall.

'Listen to me,' he said softly, his hot breath flickering against her skin. 'I will not be played games with, do you understand? Don't try to tease me. I'm not some callow boy to come begging.'

'How dare you accuse me of teasing you?' she demanded in a shaking voice.

'You're up to something. I'm not a fool, Circe.'

'And neither am I. You set Gino on to me, remember? How stupid do you think I am? Now, will you let me go?' She tried to push his arm away but it was like steel across her chest, not pressing her, but implacable.

'Not yet. We have things to talk about,' he said, speaking in the same low voice that sent warmth scurrying across her skin.

'I can't think what.' She tried to keep calm but the powerful body holding her still was communicating its heat to her, and that was mingling with the rising excitement inside herself.

'You did very well tonight,' he murmured.

'I don't know what you mean.'

'Yes, you do. You were subtle, very subtle. Nothing obvious. Just be nice to the brute and watch him melt. And you came close, until you over reached yourself.'

There was a sudden fierce note in his voice.

'Every man has to want you, doesn't he? Gino satisfies your vanity, the man in London satisfies your ambition. And me? What would I satisfy?'

His words were like hot lava pouring over her, illuminating the world, so that for a searing moment she knew the answer to his question. He would satisfy a deep, aching need that had been there, unacknowledged, in her loins, from the very start.

How long could she have gone on refusing to see it if he hadn't forced it on her?

But hell would freeze over before she would let him suspect.

'You flatter yourself,' she snapped. 'If you weren't so

conceited you'd remember I didn't say a word to you that I couldn't have said in front of Gino.'

'I've already admitted that you were clever. Far too clever to be blatant. Circe weaves her spells and has a different face for all of us. Subtlety wouldn't work with Gino, *but it damned near worked with me.*'

She didn't answer. Words would no longer come. A warm languor pervaded her, making her limbs heavy and her senses vague. Yet she was burningly aware of the faint touch of his lips against the skin of her neck.

Pride made her turn her head away but there was no escaping him. Putting her hands on his shoulders she tried to push him off, with no success.

He didn't try to kiss her mouth, merely rested his lips against her throat, then just beneath her ears, causing a storm inside her that was almost alarming in its violence.

He was warning her not to take him on, because if she did, this was what he could do to her. He could make her flesh defy her mind, defy her very self. He could make her want him when she was determined not to. He was daring her to risk it.

Either the heat of the night or her own feverish urgency was making her react in a way she didn't recognise. It took all her strength not to yearn towards him, seeking new and more deeply intimate caresses.

She could not allow this to happen, but it was happening anyway. There was danger everywhere, but suddenly danger was her natural element. The hands she'd raised to push him away changed course and curved, almost touching him but not quite.

But then—yes—her fingers just brushed his neck of their own accord. There was no stopping them. And his lips were on her face, not kissing her mouth, kissing everywhere else, driving her wild with soft, teasing caresses that left her unsatisfied because she they made her want so much more.

They were no longer alone in the street. A laughing, singing crowd swirled by, but nobody took any notice of them. One more pair of lovers among so many!

He drew back a few inches and stopped, breathing hard, his mouth close to hers. He could see her reaction, she thought desperately. There was no hiding the rise and fall of her breasts under the thin red silk, or the pulse beating in her throat. He must be able to feel her breath against his face, as heated as his own.

'Get—away—from—me,' she gasped in a voice that shook.

He did so, stepping back sharply. She saw his face, one instant before the shutters came down, and saw it ravaged, burningly intense.

And afraid. It was too late for him to lock her out and he knew it.

He turned and strode away toward the main street, leaving her leaning against the wall, trying to calm down. After a moment Alex followed him slowly.

When she had nearly reached the Piazza, Gino came flying to meet her, flowers in his hair, not entirely sober. He embraced her eagerly.

'There you are, *carissima*. Why aren't you with Rinaldo? Don't tell me you two are fighting again?'

Alex never forgot the journey home, with Rinaldo driving the car and herself and Gino in the back. Gino was too sleepy to talk, which was a relief, but left her staring out into the darkness, accompanied by thoughts that she didn't want to think.

As soon as they reached the house she bid the brothers a brief goodnight and went upstairs. She needed to be alone to control her feelings, and to understand exactly what those feelings were.

There was anger, partly at him and partly at herself for being caught off guard.

It had been there all the time. Desire. Basic, brutal, almost uncontrollable desire, not connected to any sympathy of mind. Uncivilised. Alien to her well-ordered world. The kind of feeling that she had never really believed existed, waiting to spring out and make a fool of her.

And what a fool! She could have screamed as she realised how evident her excitement must have been. He had made her want him, and he'd known it.

She closed her eyes, fiercely willing herself to hold onto the anger, so that it might defend her from the other feeling, the shattering awareness that tonight she had been alive in every part of herself, truly alive for the first time.

She didn't want to feel like that about Rinaldo, and she would resist it with everything in her power. She pulled herself together. It would be over soon. This was an aberration, that would be forgotten when she returned to England and reality.

A freezing shower made her feel a little better. Then, as she wrapped a towel around her, she grew suddenly alert, wondering what had happened to her wits. The date of the carnival had always seemed familiar, and now she knew why. This was the day of the partners' meeting, at which David would arrange for her to be offered a partnership.

It must have happened this afternoon. He'd probably been trying to get through to her ever since.

She could have laughed aloud at the way Italy had hypnotised her into forgetting something so important.

She had even left her mobile phone behind to go to the festival. All she had to do was check her messages.

She did so, and stared at the result.

There were no messages from David.

But there were four from her secretary at her home number.

She thought of Jenny, a motherly woman and a tireless worker, of whom she was very fond. Why was she making such attempts to contact her when David was silent?

Perhaps the other partners had been awkward about accepting her, and even now David was arguing with them, defending her.

She dialled Jenny's number quickly, and was answered at once.

'Thank goodness you called,' Jenny said in a relieved voice. 'You're not going to believe what I have to tell you. Are you sitting down?'

'Sure. I'm sitting on the bed. Now, tell me.'

'This afternoon David announced his engagement to Erica.'

In the first moment of shock Alex said the only words that came into her head.

'Who the blue blazes is Erica?'

'His secretary. It's funny how nobody knows her name, but that's what she's like. Little brown mouse. Fades into the wallpaper.'

Now Alex remembered a pale, wispy girl she had sometimes seen in David's office. And this little nonentity had ousted the glamorous, high-powered Alex Dacre?

'There's something else,' Jenny said. 'David has vetoed your partnership.'

Alex uttered a very rude word.

'There was a meeting this afternoon. Everyone thought

making you a partner was just a formality, but he wouldn't consider it.'

'What?'

'He said they couldn't rely on someone who stayed away so long—'

'But he told me to stay as long as I needed!'

'I know. We all know. Nobody believes it for a moment. It's just an excuse. He says you can stay on as an employee—'

'He knows I won't do that,' Alex snapped.

'Right. He doesn't want you around after the way he's treated you. He can't fire you, but he can make your life uncomfortable until you leave.'

'What would he have done if I hadn't obligingly come to Italy?' Alex asked grimly.

'He'd have thought of something. His kind always do. But you made it easy for him. All your accounts have been assigned to other people now. Officially it's "during your absence", but—'

'But I'll never get them back. Damn him! Half those accounts only came to the firm because I went out and fought for them.'

'I know, and he hates that. You've become too strong. You've become competition, and David's a very vain man.'

'Thanks for putting me in the picture Jenny,' Alex said, breathing hard.

'What are you going to do?'

'I'm going to plan my revenge in the dark.'

'What?' Jenny gave a gasp of shock.

'I'm part Italian, don't forget. We plot in the night and we keep our stilettos shining. Perhaps you should tell him that. It might give him a sleepless moment or two.'

'Oh, Alex, I know you must be terribly hurt, but is he really worth it?'

'No. I'll call again later.'

When she'd hung up Alex was still for a long time.

In truth, she wasn't hurt at all. She'd agreed David wasn't worth it and it was true. She'd blinded herself to his true nature, but at heart she'd always known the kind of man he was, cool, self-centred, ruthless where his own interests were concerned.

It hadn't mattered because she had believed herself to be the same.

But she knew better now.

She could have laughed aloud at the thought of mourning the loss of David.

Here was the true reason why he'd been so understanding about her prolonged absence. It had exactly suited him. He must have been planning to oust her from the firm even before she left.

She would waste no time in grieving, but swallowing the insult was another matter.

She noticed a small clay figurine by the side of the bed. The next moment the room shuddered under the impact as it hit the far wall and smashed.

She regarded the damage, feeling a great deal better.

'Alex! Are you all right?'

Gino was knocking on her door, calling her.

'I'm fine,' she called out, hurriedly putting on a light dressing gown.

She opened the door. Rinaldo was there too, in the background, but it was Gino who stormed in, grasping her hands, and saying, 'What was the noise? Did something fall? Are you hurt?'

She freed herself and picked up some of the pieces.

'It was only this,' she said.

Rinaldo came in and examined the dent in the wall.

'Impressive,' he said. 'You must have thrown it with some force. Remind me to duck.'

'Don't worry, I'm not aiming anything at you.'

'No, you wouldn't have missed me, would you?'

'Stop trying to provoke me,' Alex said, feeling strangely calm now that she'd gotten it out of her system. 'I'm sorry for the damage to your wall.'

'Was there any special reason for the violence?' Rinaldo asked, 'or did you just feel that way?'

She looked at him, her eyes kindling.

'I just felt that way.'

Nothing on earth would have persuaded her to tell him the truth at that moment.

Gino was alone in the kitchen, tucking into a hearty breakfast when she went down next morning. Alex regarded him sardonically, amused to see that he could hardly meet her eye.

'"I shall dance only with you, *amor mia*",' she tossed his words lightly back at him. '"*And you must dance only with me.*"'

'I know, I know,' he said shamefacedly. 'It was festival. I got carried away—'

'Yes, I saw you being carried away—by three of them. Naturally you couldn't resist.'

He eyed her suspiciously.

'Are you being very nice, or should I prepare for boiling oil to drop on my head?'

'You'll have to wait and see,' she teased.

He seized her hand and kissed it. 'I adore you.'

'No you don't. You adore your three companions of last night. At least, there were three that I saw, but I wouldn't be surprised if—'

'Yes, well never mind that,' he said hastily. 'Truly, *carissima*, it meant nothing. That's how festival is, all those demons and goats—'

'And the wine,' she said, smiling at him fondly.

'Well, the wine plays its part, but it's mostly the atmosphere—the feeling that anything could happen, and you're going to let it happen, and who knows how the evening will end?'

Alex was silent. Gino's words struck home in way he could never imagine. Last night's feeling of heated sexuality had pervaded her too, giving everything a sharper edge, making her feel things it might have been better not to feel, and even rejoice in them.

But now it was the clear light of day.

'I'm sorry,' he said, seeing her face and misreading it. 'I shouldn't have said that.'

'Why not? I do understand. It was festival. You never stick with the person you came with. Otherwise it's no fun.'

'Bless you for a sweet, forgiving darling.'

He planted a swift kiss on her mouth, and Alex let him. It wasn't unpleasant. It wasn't anything.

'You know I adore you more than life, don't you?' he asked. 'You're the one I dream of—'

'Except during a festival,' she couldn't resist saying.

'Can we put that behind us?' he asked, harassed.

'I'm sorry, Gino dear, but I can't help laughing. You're such a ham.'

'I bare my heart to you and you laugh,' he said plaintively. 'Ah, well!' He struck his breast theatrically. '*Ridi, pagliacco, ridi!* Laugh, clown, laugh, though your heart is breaking.'

'Clown is right,' Alex said severely.

Then, with a quick change of mood that was one of

his characteristics, Gino said, 'Don't go back to England, Alex.'

'Gino—'

'You've changed since coming here. I'll bet you don't even recognise yourself any more.'

It was true. Gino's perceptions could be disconcerting, but she wasn't ready to trust him with the truth any more than Rinaldo.

'You can't return to that other life,' Gino urged. 'You don't belong there any more.'

To throw him off the scent she quickly resumed her bantering tone.

'You stop that. I told you, I see through your little schemes.'

'Please, *cara*—' he begged in comical dismay.

'You're as bad as Rinaldo. The two of you set it all up before I arrived. I wouldn't put it past you to have tossed a coin for me.'

It was a passing remark but Gino's alarmed gulp told her everything.

'You *did*!' she accused.

'Yes—no—it wasn't like that.'

'I'll bet it was exactly like that. You cheeky pair!'

'You're not annoyed?'

'I ought to be, but oh, what the heck! I suppose I should just be glad you won.'

Emboldened by her matter-of-fact attitude Gino grinned and said, 'Actually I didn't.'

'*What?*'

'Rinaldo won, but he didn't take it seriously. He claimed he thought I'd been using my two-headed coin or he wouldn't have played. Anyway, he said he wasn't interested and I could have you.'

'Oh, really!' she asked in a dangerously quiet voice.

'But aren't you glad you got me instead? Come on, admit it. You like me better than Rinaldo.'

'I like anybody better than Rinaldo.'

'I behaved badly, leaving you with him last night, didn't I? I'm sorry if he offended you.'

'*I* may have offended *him*,' she said vaguely.

'I wonder if that's why he's gone.'

'What?'

'Yes, he left early this morning. Something about checking out some second-hand farm machinery, but I didn't know we needed any. He just upped and went.'

She should have been glad of the breathing space. Instead she felt as though she'd been dealt a blow.

They had unfinished business. Rinaldo knew that as well as she did. And he'd simply gone off and left her stranded in limbo. For a moment she looked around for something else to throw.

Then she forced herself to calm down and conceal the storm inside. That must remain her secret until she understood herself better.

She took a horse and rode for miles, noticing how the corn had grown since she first saw it, how the olives and grapes were flourishing in the sun.

How she loved the sun! It was as though she had only discovered it in Italy. There was sun in London, but it beat down in fierce strips of ugly road, baking pavements, suffocating. Here sunshine was fresh air and freedom, and a new awakening.

Her options were simple. She could return to England and fight, or she could stay here and fight. It was fighting either way, no question.

The prizes were uneven. A cold, soulless place in the firm, or another firm. There were plenty who would be glad to have her.

Or she could abandon London and everything she had worked for. All those years of striving for the best, the best clients, the best apartment, the best clothes, the best invitations—all gone to nothing.

In exchange she would have a life here, in a country that had seized her heart, in daily contact with a man who was rude, hostile, unrelenting, a man who'd rejected her out of hand without even seeing her, but who also troubled her heart and her restless body.

'Nonsense!' she said aloud. 'I'm damned if I'm going to fall in love with him! *Who the hell does he think he is?*'

After a while she made up her mind. It felt less like taking a decision than facing the inevitable. Mounting her horse she galloped back to the farm and began to pack. The following morning, in the teeth of Gino's protests, she drove herself to the airport.

There she handed the car in at the local branch of the rental company. An hour later she was in the air, on her way to England.

Rinaldo was away for a week. Twice he called and left messages on the answerphone. Eventually the phone was answered by Teresa, who brought him up to date with events, including the fact that Alex had left and would not be returning.

The following evening Rinaldo arrived home.

He found Gino sitting at the desk in his office, frowning as he poured over account books.

'You'll never manage it,' he said, grinning. 'Give up.'

'*Rinaldo!*' Gino leapt to his feet and hugged his brother eagerly.

Rinaldo hugged him back, and for a moment the two brothers thumped each other on the back.

'What's been happening?' Rinaldo asked.

'Alex has gone,' Gino said gloomily.

'So I gather from Teresa.'

'Is that all you've got to say?' Gino demanded, outraged.

'What do you want me to say? She was always bound to go back where she belongs.'

'I felt she belonged here,' Gino sighed.

'That's what she wanted you to think, to keep you off guard. Circe played her games, and we were nearly fooled. Forget her.'

'You as good as told me to make love to her.'

'Yes, and I should have known better. You're no match for her. It's lucky you didn't fall for her seriously.'

'Who says I didn't?'

'You forget how well I know you. Your most death-defying passion lasted a whole two days, I seem to recall.'

Gino shrugged despondently. 'Yeah—well, she's gone now.'

'So forget her.'

'Do you think she really loves him?'

'I said forget her.'

'Hey!' Gino said, staring into Rinaldo's tense face. 'No need to get mad at me.'

'I'm sorry,' Rinaldo growled, rubbing his eyes. 'I've had a long drive, and I'm not in the best of moods.'

'You do look pretty done in,' Gino said with his quick sympathy.

In fact, he thought, his brother looked as though he hadn't slept for a week. Or if he had slept, he'd had nightmares.

Poor old fellow, Gino thought. The threat to the farm must be troubling him more than he let on.

'Come and have something to eat,' he said kindly. 'And you can tell me about the machinery.'

'Machinery?'

'The stuff you went to buy.'

'Oh, that. No, I didn't find anything. Something to eat sounds a good idea.'

The maids had already gone to bed. Teresa served them in the kitchen, then retired.

Gino noticed that Rinaldo ate as though he barely knew what the food was.

'So what have you been doing these last few days?' he asked.

'Oh—driving around.'

'For a week?'

'Am I accountable to you?'

'If I vanished for a week I'd have some explaining to do.'

'So you would. Now drop it and tell me the news. When did Alex leave?'

'The day after you did. I keep waiting to hear from the lawyers, but nothing's happened.'

'We'll hear when it suits her,' Rinaldo observed. 'She's playing games.'

That was the mantra he'd repeated obsessively during the last few days. She was playing games, which meant he'd done the right thing to get the hell out.

From that first startling moment at his father's funeral he'd known that he couldn't afford to weaken where this woman was concerned. Hard on the heels of that thought had come fierce regret that he'd 'given' her to Gino. He'd said it casually, arrogantly, thinking life was that simple. In truth he'd expected a female dragon who would scare his volatile brother off.

Then he'd met her and known that this was a job for a man, not a boy.

Their antagonism was a relief, giving him a breathing space. But she'd been clever, offering sympathy like water in a desert to a man who'd spent too long being strong for others. The feeling was so good that he'd almost weakened, but he'd escaped in time.

So he'd won, as he made sure he always did. But now he found himself in a wilderness, his victory nothing but ashes.

'I don't think she was just playing games,' Gino said quietly.

'Then why is she back in England now, planning her wedding?'

Gino had no answer. Looking at the weariness in Rinaldo's face made him realise how depressed were his own spirits. The house had been quiet since Alex left, life had lost its savour.

After that there seemed nothing to say. Rinaldo fetched a bottle of old malt whisky, and they sat in companionable silence, sipping slowly, until Gino roused himself to say in a diffident voice.

'There's something I've been wanting to ask you for a while now.'

'Go on.'

'The day Poppa died—you were at the hospital first. By the time I arrived, it was too late. And I always wondered—what happened?'

'Nothing, he was unconscious.'

'I know but—he didn't come round?—even for a moment?'

'If he had I'd have told you.'

'It's just so hard to think of him just lying there, still

alive but not talking.' Gino sighed ruefully. 'You know what a talker he was.'

Rinaldo closed his eyes, and through his memory there passed the picture of his father, terribly still, swathed in bandages.

Like Gino he had felt it impossible that a man so full of life could lie still and silent. At any moment he would open his eyes, recognise his son and speak. There would be—there *must* be, some exchange between them before the end.

The picture swirled, blurred. He struggled to see clearly again but it was gone. As often before, he was tortured by the feeling of something there, just beyond the edge of memory.

Several times in the past he had come to the edge of this moment, but whatever it was always eluded him, driven away by the jangle in his head.

It had happened that day in the barn with Alex. Their brief moment of sympathy had caused a door of memory to start opening. But not far enough. And it would never happen again now. She had gone, and that was all for the best.

He would try to believe it.

'I wish I had something to tell you,' he said heavily. 'I, too, find it hard that he just left us without a word of goodbye or explanation. But there's nothing we can do but accept it. Now let's get some sleep.'

They went upstairs to bed, and the house lay in silence for an hour. Then Gino awoke, uncertain why, but with a feeling that something was up.

Pulling on a robe he slipped into the corridor, where he found Rinaldo, dressed in shorts.

'We have a burglar downstairs,' Rinaldo said softly.

On bare feet they moved noiselessly along the corridor

and down the stairs. Through the door they could make out part of the room illuminated by a bar of moonlight. The rest was in darkness, but they could hear the intruder moving about, then a crash, like a chair overturning.

'Right,' Rinaldo muttered.

He moved fast, not switching on the light but judging the position by sound alone, then launching himself forward, colliding with a body that reeled back, landing on the floor beneath him.

For a moment they fought in silence, gasping with effort and writhing madly together. Gino, coming into the room, heard a yell from Rinaldo as something caught him on the side of the head. Hurriedly Gino put the light on.

Then he froze at the sight that met his eyes.

Rinaldo drew in a sharp breath. 'You!' he said explosively.

From her position on the floor Alex glared up at him. *'Get—off—me!'* she said emphatically.

Breathing hard, Rinaldo pulled back from her, and stood up. Alex rose stiffly, supporting herself on Gino's outstretched hand.

'What the devil are you doing here?' Rinaldo demanded.

'I live here. I went away, now I've come back.'

'I knew you wouldn't just leave us and forget,' Gino breathed joyfully.

'When I left I didn't know what was going to happen,' Alex said. 'I had to see how the land lay. Now I know, and I'm here to stay.'

'What does the English fiancé have to say about that?' Rinaldo demanded, rubbing his face self-consciously. 'Can we look forward to his descent on us? Shall I tell Teresa to prepare a room for him? Perhaps you mean to be married from this house?'

'Oh, put a sock in it,' Alex said firmly.

'Excuse me? Sock?'

'It's an English expression,' she explained. 'It means don't say any more. David's out of the picture.'

'You dumped him?' Gino cried joyfully.

'No, he dumped me. I found out on the night of the festival that he'd vetoed my partnership and got engaged to his mousy secretary. I went back to England to have the satisfaction of telling him a few home truths, face to face.'

'I'll wager you did it in great style,' Rinaldo observed.

'Oh, I did. In front of everyone. I can't tell you how much I enjoyed that. My lawyer will go after the firm for a settlement. I've put my apartment on the market, and after that there was nothing left to do but come back here.'

'You couldn't have notified us that you were arriving, in a sensible, civilised manner?' Rinaldo observed.

'Where's the fun in that? Actually, I didn't mean to be so late, but I had to pick up the car I've bought on the way and that delayed me.

'I didn't mean to awaken you, so I arrived as quietly as I could. I didn't slam the door when I got out, and I climbed in by that window over there, the one that doesn't close properly.

'So here I am. This is my home too now. Get used to me, gentlemen, because I've come to stay.'

CHAPTER NINE

SOME women would have splashed out on a new wardrobe. Alex had splashed out on a car that reduced both brothers to awed silence. It managed to be stylish, glossily expensive and 'heavy-duty' at the same time.

'How much?' Rinaldo murmured.

'More than I could afford,' Alex said happily.

'I take my hat off to you.'

The car declared that she had come to stay, big time. She'd already said so in words, but this affirmed it.

'I'm going to drive a lot over the next week or so,' she said. 'I want to see every single part of Belluna. You don't mind, do you?'

'I have no right to mind.'

His tone was impeccably polite, but she would have preferred the knockabout that she had become used to. Since her return both men seemed to be treating her with kid gloves. Gino's manner was gentle, Rinaldo's was wary.

She began to study Belluna at close quarters. The year was moving on and it would soon be time for harvest. Wherever she went she found people who knew about her through the grapevine, and who treated her with cautious respect until they discovered that she knew a little Tuscan. Then there were smiles, laughter at her mistakes, eagerness to teach her.

One of her most enjoyable moments came when she returned from a trip to find Rinaldo standing by the side of the road next to his broken-down car.

It was rare for him to dress 'for best'. Old shirt and shabby jeans were his normal attire around the farm. But now he wore a charcoal suit that was both elegant and fashionable, plus a tie.

His hair was brushed and tidy, and he looked almost like a different man. A handsome man, with and 'air', an extra something that most men did not have. Combined with the authority that was natural to him, it made him startlingly attractive. Alex felt a soft thud in the pit of her stomach.

She drew up and sat waiting at the wheel as he approached.

'If you dare laugh—' he growled.

'Nothing was further from my thoughts,' she said untruthfully. 'Is the break-down truck on its way?'

'No, because I came out without my phone today. I'm warning you—' Her lips had twitched.

'Don't get stroppy with me,' she advised him, 'or I'll drive off and leave you here.'

'No, you won't,' he said unexpectedly. 'You'd never sink that low.'

'I could try and force myself,' she said, getting out of the car and heading for the boot. 'But I have towing gear, and it seems a shame to waste it.'

They recovered the equipment from the boot of her car.

'You'd better keep back and let me do the work,' she told him. 'Or you might spoil your suit.'

His answer was to strip off his jacket and shirt.

He shouldn't have done that, she thought, not when she was trying to concentrate on what she was doing. How was she supposed to keep her mind on work when he was standing there, the sun burnishing his torso?

She guessed he must work like this a good deal, for

the tan was even all over his broad back, shoulders and chest. With his tall figure and powerful neck, he looked exactly what he was, a forceful, virile male. And she was supposed to think about towing gear. There was no justice in the world.

She forced her attention back to the work, managing to do her full share, moving deftly and skilfully.

'I see you know what you're doing,' he said.

'If you'd experienced as much prejudice about women drivers as I have, you'd make sure you could do things for yourself, as well,' she informed him. 'The garages are the worst. They assume you're an idiot. One manager told me to bring my husband in and he'd explain it. In this day and age! Oh, heck!'

The exclamation was drawn from her by her hair flopping over her forehead. It was years since she'd needed to brush back her hair, but these days it seemed to happen all the time.

How long had it been since she'd visited a hair salon? Instead of being immaculately styled and coiffed, her hair had grown, becoming almost shaggy. When she finished work and stood up, the slight breeze made it blow about her face.

He replaced his clothes and got into the passenger seat.

'Where shall I take you?' she asked when they were on the road.

'There's a garage halfway to Florence that will repair the car. When we've dropped it there I need to go into the city to keep an appointment. I'll get a taxi home.'

'I don't mind waiting for you. I can do some shopping.'

'There's no need,' he said briefly.

'Oh, I see. Like that.'

'What do you mean, like that?'

'You know what I mean. You don't want me to know where you're going. I expect it's a secret assignation with a mystery woman—'

'Why would it have to be a secret? I'm a free agent. I do as I please.'

'Well, perhaps she isn't the only one,' she said, wishing he would deny it.

'You could have a whole harem dotted around Florence,' she persisted when he stayed silent. 'Or maybe—'

'I'm visiting the accountant.'

It took a moment to subdue the flicker of pleasure that he wasn't visiting a woman. When she was sure she could speak steadily she said,

'Ah! Yes, I understand. You're afraid I'll want to come too.'

'And I'm sure you will,' he said with a sigh of resignation.

'Well, I might drop in, just to do you a favour.'

He ground his teeth. 'Turn off here for the garage.'

He could be as grumpy as he liked, she thought. Nothing could quell the feeling that surged over her. She didn't analyse it, but it felt alarmingly like joy simply because he was here. She tried to file it away to be examined later, but it wouldn't be sidelined so easily.

When they'd delivered the car to the garage she swung back onto the road to Florence.

'Where am I heading?' she asked, as they entered the city.

'The Via Bonifacio Lupi. His name is Enrico Varsi.'

'Is it all right if I come in with you?'

'You're *asking* me?'

'I'm asking you.'

'And if I say no?'

'Then I'll wait meekly outside. But I'll put arsenic in your soup.'

He didn't reply, and she couldn't take her eyes off the road, but she knew, with total certainty, that he was grinning.

It was the area of Florence where lawyers and accountants congregated, a place of sedate streets and decorum. Alex had to park a little way up the road and walk back, studying the plaques by the doors. One, in particular, caught her attention, causing her to stop and study it for so long that Rinaldo had to call out,

'If you don't come now I shall go in without you.'

She scurried to catch up. 'You gave in,' she teased.

She could have sworn he ground his teeth. 'I did not give in, I merely recognise that you have certain financial rights, and I wish to behave properly.'

'Same thing,' she jeered.

'Get in there before I strangle you.'

Signor Varsi's offices were luxurious, the surroundings of a very successful man. He spoke well, covering complex matters without needing to refer to notes, and was clearly master of his material.

He behaved perfectly to her, showing the professional courtesy of one accountant to another. He did not talk down to her, and several times invited her opinion. She said as little as possible but her ears were pricked for anything she could learn.

Afterwards she and Rinaldo went for a coffee near the Duomo.

'You're very thoughtful,' he said, glancing at her face.

'I'm fascinated by the discovery that the Italian financial year runs from January the first to December the thirty-first.'

'But of course it does,' he said, puzzled. 'What else could it be?'

'In my country it's April to April.'

'And the British have the nerve to call Italians an illogical race?'

'I know.' She gave a brief laugh and went back to staring into her coffee.

'Alex, are you all right?'

His unusually gentle tone made her look up. His was looking at her with grave concern that had no hint of irony or suspicion.

'How do you mean—all right?'

'You've lost the man you loved. You don't let anyone see that you mind. You smile at Gino and me, you make jokes, and anyone who didn't know you would think everything was fine in your world.'

'Do you think you know me?'

'As much as you'll let me. And I know that you can't really be as bright and cheerful as you seem. You've given me a shoulder to cry on in the past.'

Looking into his eyes she saw kindness, something she had never found there before. The sight was almost her undoing.

'I'm not crying,' she said huskily.

'Most women would be after their fiancé dumped them for another woman.'

'There's no need to make me sound like a weeping wallflower,' she protested with a shaky laugh.

'No, you're no weeping wallflower. In fact, I can't imagine you ever weeping. You're too strong.'

'Strong? Are you sure you don't mean hard?'

'I might have thought so once. But not now. You have a deep-feeling heart, but you guard it carefully.'

'As you do yourself.'

'Yes,' he said after a moment. 'As I do myself. I think we've both learned to be cautious. But feelings have to be expressed one way, if not another. I still remember that dent in the wall.'

'Dent—? Oh, you mean when I threw the ornament?'

'That was why you did it, wasn't it?'

'Yes,' she said ruefully.

'So you are an Italian deep inside, after all? The woman who arrived here wouldn't have chucked things, merely uttered a few well-chosen words.'

'I wasn't quite as cool and collected as I seemed in those days,' she admitted, 'but I did feel that things could usually be sorted out with reason.'

She gave a brief inner smile, aimed at herself and the person she had been. How little reason seemed to matter, sitting here with the man who brought her to life as she had never thought to be.

'And now?' he asked.

'Let's just say that I'm having a re-think. There are times when a rush of blood to the head can be very satisfying.'

He grinned. 'Your mother would be proud of you.'

'Yes, she would,' Alex said, realising that it was true. She gave a crack of laughter. 'She'd have done exactly what I did. Oh, Mamma, I wish you could see me now.'

'What did she think of your fiancé?'

'She didn't like him. She said he was too organised.'

'A virtue, surely, in his profession? And yours.'

'Yes, but it's not just in his profession,' Alex mused. 'Everything in his life was organised, I see that now.'

She wasn't looking at Rinaldo, but at the tablecloth as she moved spoons back and forth into patterns.

'We had it all planned,' she said thoughtfully. 'Our home, our marriage, the way our professional lives would entwine. Married to each other, we'd have dominated the firm. Of course, that was what he didn't want. He wants to dominate it alone. I thought we loved each other, but all that time he was secretly planning to ease me out in any way he could. I guess he couldn't believe his luck when I came out here.'

She shook her head over her own naïvety. 'Lord, but I made it easy for him!'

'Because you trusted him,' Rinaldo suggested.

'Oh, yes. Conspicuous trustworthiness is David's big asset. It's worth at least thirty per cent on the bill.'

She knew she sounded bitter, but she couldn't help it. Fool! she thought. Fool to have been so deluded for so long!

'How long did you know him?' Rinaldo asked.

'Years. He was there the day I joined the firm, when I was little more than a kid. I supposed I hero-worshipped him, chiefly because he was so good-looking. It took a long time for us to come together.'

'You're very focused.'

'Decide what you want and go for it. That's me.'

'And what do you want now?' he asked, watching her.

'I don't know. For the first time in my life I don't know what I want. I feel cast adrift.'

'Yet you seem as sure of yourself as ever, Circe.'

'That's really unfair,' she said, smiling wistfully. 'Did it ever occur to you that Circe was a very confused person?'

'She wasn't a person, she was a goddess, an enchantress.'

'A witch,' she reminded him.

'A witch,' he agreed. 'But a witch who sows confusion all around her.'

'I never meant to. But you and I had such preconceived

ideas about each other. There was bound to be confusion.'

He nodded. 'No more preconceived ideas, I swear. I'll never again see you as an automaton who thinks only cold reason matters.'

'Can I have that in writing?' she asked sceptically.

'No, I'll just have to prove it to you.'

'For that, I'll let you drive the car home,' she said, handing him the keys.

He pocketed them. 'Is this you being sweetly feminine?'

'Nope. I'm just tired. You can do the work.'

Laughing they made their way through the streets in the direction of the car.

'I haven't abandoned reason altogether,' she hastened to say. 'But I've come to see that it can sometimes be overrated.'

'Only sometimes?'

'It has its place, even for you. You were very reasonable in Varsi's office.'

A noisy vehicle rumbled by as he answered, and Alex couldn't make out his reply distinctly. She gave herself a little shake, trying to believe that he had really said, *'But I don't want to kiss Enrico Varsi.'*

'What did you say?' she asked, dazed.

'I said we turn here,' he said quickly.

Strangely his denial convinced her. He might pretend what he liked. He'd said it. Suddenly she wanted this afternoon to last for ever.

He was silent on the journey home, and Alex was also content to say nothing. Something was happening that words would only spoil.

*   *   *

Later that evening, in the quiet of her room, Alex called Jenny, her one-time secretary.

'I'm afraid I'm useless as a source of info,' Jenny told her. 'I've walked out of the firm. If I'd had to look at David's smug face any longer I'd have done something to it. But I'll always be glad I was there when you told him "what for" in front of everyone.'

'Yes, I enjoyed it too,' Alex mused. 'But I'm sorry you're out of a job.'

'I'm not. I've gone to—' she named another firm, equally prestigious, just across the street. 'I think they'd quite like to have you as well.'

'I'm glad you're suited, but I have a job to do here. Jenny, does the name Andansio mean anything to you?'

'I remember it from about five years ago, before I became your secretary. My then boss had some dealings with them.'

'What can you tell me about them?'

'A lot. Some of it's quite sensational.'

Alex listened for half an hour, making notes. When she hung up she was thoughtful.

A few days later, Varsi's secretary called to say that the books were ready to be returned, and should they be mailed? It was Alex who took the call, and volunteered to collect them. On her way out she met Rinaldo and told him her errand.

'And of course you'll deliver them to me without looking at them?' he said ironically.

'Did I say that?' she asked, wide-eyed with innocence.

'Well at least you play fair,' he said appreciatively.

Having got the books, Alex shut herself up with them for several hours.

'I notice that most of the pages were printed then put in ring-binders later,' she said to Rinaldo.

'My father used a computer for the accounts,' he said. 'He was very proud of the fact that he'd mastered it.'

'Can I see his files?'

Rinaldo showed her into the study, switched on the computer and showed her what she needed. Then he left her.

Alex's first impression was that Poppa's pride had been well-founded. Comparing his files to the receipts she came to the conclusion that he'd kept his records perfectly. They were detailed, informative and easy to check.

Next she managed to access files for previous years, and, after a search, located the books that matched them. She spent a long night checking and cross-checking.

It was early morning by the time she'd finished and switched off the computer. Instead of going to bed she put on her work-out clothes and went running. Then she showered, ate a swift breakfast, and drove into Florence.

She began spending lengthy periods in the city, sometimes driving back late at night, sometimes staying in a hotel. Without saying very much she gave the brothers the impression that she was enjoying a pleasure trip, shopping and going to the theatre. Rinaldo occasionally gave her puzzled glances, but he held his peace.

Soon there was no time for questions, for the harvest was due to begin. Wheat, olives, lemons, now ripe under the burning sun, had to be brought in, stored and sold to the waiting markets.

'And after them, the wine,' Gino told her. 'Maybe October.'

'Maybe? You don't know?'

'Judging the right moment for picking grapes can be

very tricky. You have to wait until they're sweet enough, or you can end up with vinegar. Try this.'

They were sitting on the veranda enjoying the last of the sun. On the low table between them was a bunch of deep purple grapes that he had picked that afternoon. He took one, peeled it carefully with a tiny knife, and offered it to her.

'Sweet?' he asked.

'It tastes very sweet.'

'But not quite sweet enough. It needs more than this before it's ready.'

'And you can tell the moment by the taste.'

'Rinaldo can, he's the real expert. He says he's never wrong. Mind you, he thinks that about everything.'

'Talking about me?' came Rinaldo's voice from just inside the house.

He came out and pulled up another chair, acknowledging Alex with only a brief nod, but sitting close to her. It was the first time she had seen him all day.

'I was just explaining to Alex how you value your taste buds above the achievements of science.'

'What has science got to do with it?' Alex wanted to know.

'Nothing,' Rinaldo said. 'Judging grapes is an art. You either have it or you haven't. And my little brother hasn't, so he tries to pretend that science is the next best thing.'

'No, it's the very *best* thing,' Gino said stubbornly.

'But what science?' Alex asked, baffled.

From his pocket Gino pulled a narrow metal tube, about six inches long. It reminded Alex of a small telescope, except that at one end was a piece of yellow glass that lifted, revealing a small box beneath.

Into this Gino inserted a grape and closed the lid, squashing the grape so that the juice flowed.

'Now look,' he said, holding it up.

Alex squinted from the other end and saw a tiny dial. The needle was hovering back and forth, almost near the red area, but not quite settling there.

'It tells you the sugar content,' Gino explained. 'When that's right, you know it's time to pick.'

Rinaldo gave a snort of contempt.

'I've known you use it,' Gino protested. 'When it suited you.'

'I've occasionally demonstrated that it backs me up,' Rinaldo agreed.

'And when it doesn't, you ignore it.'

'Yes, because I know grapes better than any machine. That's enough talk. I'm going to bed. If you're wise, you will too. We have a long, hard haul ahead of us.'

Just how hard a haul Alex was to discover. Both Rinaldo and Gino played their full part in the harvest, often picking with their own hands. Alex plunged in, determined to earn her place here by hard work as well as money.

Even she, inexperienced, knew that this would be a good harvest. The long, hot summer had brought the crops to perfection at exactly the right moment, until at last only the grapes were left.

'And we start on those tomorrow,' Rinaldo said.

The three of them were sitting on the veranda, in various stages of exhaustion. Gino was sprawled in his chair, his head right back. But he lifted it when he heard this.

'Tomorrow?' he echoed. 'You can't mean that.'

'I do mean it. The grapes are ready.'

'Not according to this.' Gino lifted the instrument that was used for testing the grapes, which was lying on the low table.

'I don't need a machine to tell me the grapes are ready,' Rinaldo said stubbornly.

'Rinaldo be sensible.'

'Machines don't drink wine. People do. The grapes are ready.'

'But nobody else is harvesting now. They're all waiting another week.'

'Great. We'll be ahead of the market and our grapes will be the best. We'll get the highest price. I'm going to bed.'

Gino's shocked eyes followed him until he was out of sight.

'He's taken leave of his senses,' he said. 'I've never known him like this before.'

'But you said he's the real expert,' Alex reminded him. 'Has this never happened in the past?'

'Only by the odd day or two. But a week? He's never been out on that much of a limb before. What's got into him to take such a risk?'

'Is it really a great risk?'

'Being wrong by a day can take the edge of perfection off the harvest. He's risking everything.'

Risking everything. Yes, Alex thought, Rinaldo had had the air of a man leaping into the unknown, ready to chance all he had on one reckless throw of the dice.

Next day, as he'd said, the grape harvest began. The work was long and laborious, for grape picking was another task Rinaldo wouldn't entrust to machines, saying they damaged the plants.

Alex piled in, picking until her hands were sore. If she tried to talk to Rinaldo he replied automatically. Sometimes she wondered if he really knew that she was there. She had the odd sensation that he was looking beyond her.

'Pick,' he said fiercely. 'Just pick.'

She never knew how she got through that week. Somehow she'd been swept up by his own intensity, driving herself on to some unknown goal. When the last grape was in she felt drained and futile, as though the purpose of her whole life had been taken away.

The Farneses were not wine makers, but sold their grapes to a company. When Signor Valli, the company representative who always dealt with them, received their summons, he gave a yell of pleasure.

'That's great. I know we can always trust Rinaldo's palate. I'll be right over.'

Alex had meant to be there for his visit, but at the last moment she had to make one of her trips to Florence for a long talk with the accountant, Andansio. What she heard from him was absorbing, but it was still hard to concentrate when her mind was with Rinaldo, learning the result of his life or death gamble.

She wasn't sure how she knew that it was life and death. But she had no doubt of it.

It was dark when she drove home, and hurried into the house. She found the two brothers standing in silence and her heart sank.

'What is it?' she asked, looking from one to the other.

'I got it wrong,' Rinaldo said bluntly. 'The wine was harvested too soon. It needed another week. I got it wrong.'

Her heart almost stopped. His face was ravaged, as though he were dying inside. And she could feel it with him, the pain of failure and defeat, almost beyond bearing.

'But how—?' she whispered.

'Because I believed what I wanted to believe,' he said

heavily. 'People do that every day, but I've cost us the best of the wine harvest.'

'You mean it's all unusable?' Alex asked, shocked.

'Oh, no, it's not unusable,' Rinaldo said with ironic self-condemnation. 'Valli will buy the grapes, not at top prices for Chianti, but as second grade to bulk out some inferior wine.'

'That's never happened to us before,' Gino said.

He spoke softly, but Rinaldo's lacerated sensibilities made every word pierce him.

'No, it's never happened before, and it wouldn't have happened this time if I hadn't been such a blind fool. Say it.'

'You made one mistake,' Gino said kindly. 'It's not the end of the world.'

Rinaldo walked to the tall window that opened onto the veranda, and looked back. Suddenly his voice was almost that of an old man.

'You're being generous my brother, as always,' he said. 'But it *is* the end of the world. I can't explain that, but take my word for it. I need time to think. Don't follow me either of you.'

He walked out into the darkness.

CHAPTER TEN

IT WAS warm for October and Alex slept with the window open to catch any hint of breeze. Even so her sleep was restless, and at last she awoke.

Climbing out of bed she went to the open window, not troubling to cover her nakedness as there would be nobody out there to see her.

She recalled how she had looked out of this window once before and seen Rinaldo burying Brutus. That was when she had known that he had a heart. It was awkward and prickly, and would never be given easily. But it felt deeply, powerfully. Perhaps it was then she'd begun to suspect that she wanted it.

She knew it now with total certainty. It would have been an understatement to say that she loved Rinaldo. Falling in love did not begin to express the way he'd taken possession of her heart, her mind, her hopes, dreams, instincts.

The only thing he hadn't possessed was her body, and now more than ever she felt the need to lie with him, taking him into herself so that they could be one in the complete surrender of love. Then perhaps she might find the means to comfort him for the wretched failure he had brought upon himself, for reasons that she still did not understand.

She'd longed to follow him as he'd walked away into the night, but his prohibition blocked her way.

When she saw the man moving between the trees she thought her imagination was reliving that first occasion.

Then she realised that Rinaldo was really there, and in the moonlight she could just see him well enough to know that he was crushed.

She couldn't bear it. Whatever he said, she must be with him. Hurriedly she pulled on a short nightgown and a light linen robe, thrust some slippers on her feet, and was out of the door, running down the stairs.

As she reached the trees she lost sight of him, and for a moment she was afraid he might have moved on. But then she saw him, sitting on a log, his hands clasped between his knees, his head sunk in an attitude of despair.

He didn't hear her approach until she dropped down on her knees beside him.

'Rinaldo— Rinaldo—' There was so much she wanted to say, but she could speak only his name.

She put her hands on either side of his face. 'Don't turn away from me,' she begged.

He didn't try to turn away, but he sat looking at her with the saddest face she thought she had ever seen. It made Alex abandon words and pull his head down until his lips were on hers.

He almost resisted, but he had no power to hold out against her for long. The next moment his arms went about her, drawing her tightly against him in a long, fierce kiss.

She could feel his desperation and it made her wind her arms about his neck, pressing herself against him, giving to him with everything she had.

'Alex—' he tried to say.

'No,' she told him fiercely. 'Not yet.'

'Not yet,' he agreed, the words almost smothered against her mouth.

Before this he had touched her face with his lips, but he had never laid them over hers. Now he did so and the feeling was as fiercely wonderful as her dreams had promised her. He kissed her with a hard, driving urgency, as though afraid that she would be snatched away.

She responded in kind, caressing his mouth feverishly, trying to draw him on to give her what she most urgently wanted from him at this moment.

But then she felt his shoulders turn to iron beneath her hands, his whole body tensed to put a distance between them.

'Stop!' he said hoarsely. 'I must tell you something.'

'Let it wait.' She was gasping. She wanted him and words were an irrelevance that got in the way.

'No, you must hear me out first.'

She forced herself to calm down, sensing that this was vital to him. When his hands fell from her she seized them, holding them between her own.

'Tell me what it is that's making you like this,' she said. 'It can't be just the grapes.'

'You don't understand,' he said so fiercely that she was startled. 'If I'd been right, I'd have got top price and been ahead of the market. And that was what I wanted more than anything in life.

'I wanted it so much that I blinded myself to the truth. I told myself I had to be right. When I tasted those grapes I found what I wanted to find. *Idiot! Stupid, conceited clown!*'

She was shocked by the agony of self-condemnation in his voice.

'I thought I could order things to be as I wanted.' He gave a crack of mirthless laughter. 'You'd think I'd have learned better than that by now, wouldn't you?'

'Please, don't be so hard on yourself,' she begged. 'So you let your pride get in the way—'

'Not pride, arrogance. I wouldn't listen, would I? And

now I've brought down my best hopes, and damaged the farm.'

'But the rest of the harvest was good—'

'Oh, yes, we won't go under. We'll survive, but not as prosperously as we should have done, because I was blind and pig-headed—*because it mattered so much I couldn't see anything else.*'

'But what mattered that much?' she asked.

He stared. 'How can you ask? Isn't it obvious?'

'Not to me.'

'I might have wiped out my debt to you, or most of it. For weeks I've lived and breathed that. I've thought of nothing else but the moment when I could repay you.

'I told you I could have got the best price if I'd been right. And I blew it. All I can do now is pay you instalments, but I'll still be deep in your debt.'

'Oh, I see,' she said. His words had raised a hideous possibility. She had been deceiving herself. He wanted her sexually, but he'd never lost the hope of getting rid of her in the end.

'You don't see at all,' he said with soft vehemence.

'You wanted to pay me off. Then everything would have been all right, wouldn't it?'

'Yes, because then I could have said things to you that I can't say while I'm your debtor. How can a man tell a woman what she means to him when he owes her money?'

She grew still, trying to see his face in the shafts of moonlight that slanted between the trees.

'I suppose—that depends on what she means to him,' she whispered.

He touched her face. 'More than I can find words for. I've dreamed of the moment when I had no *monetary* reason for marrying you, because then you could believe

that I loved you. All this time I've wanted to say something, but I told myself it must wait until I had money.'

'To hell with your money!' she said vehemently. 'I
don't want it, I want *you*, and if you weren't blinded with
pride you'd have known that long ago.'

'Would I?' he asked with a touch of wistfulness that
sounded strange from him. 'Then perhaps I'm not a very
perceptive man.'

'There's no perhaps about it,' she breathed. 'Why must
the mortgage be so important?'

'It's important to me to come to you with my head
high.'

'You'll always have your head high. Do you think I'd
suspect you of being mercenary? How could I after you
fought so hard to drive me off?' She tried to lighten his
mood with a mild joke. 'Nobody could ever accuse you
of sweet-talking me.'

He gave a brief smile, but she could tell he was only
half ready to hear her.

'I know you're stubborn and hard and awkward,' she
said, 'but would you really turn your back on me because
of this?'

Sombrely he shook his head. 'I could never turn my
back on you,' he said in a low voice. 'I told myself I
could, but it isn't true. I *must* love you. I cannot help
myself. But I wanted it to be right between us.'

Tenderly she touched his face. 'You fool,' she said
softly. 'You dear fool, don't you know that it will be
right between us if we love each other? Not because of
money. Rinaldo, listen to me. What has money to do with
us? From the first moment it got in the way, blinding us
to what should have been obvious.'

'I know you're right. But it hurts me here—' he

pointed to his heart '—that I can't approach you as an equal.'

'Do you love me as much as I love you? Because if you do, we're equals in the only way that matters.'

'A thousand times more. I thought I was so complete in myself before you came. You showed me that I wasn't. That's why I fought you so hard. I've never fought anyone as hard as I've fought you.'

'That's how I know you love me,' she whispered.

'Ah, you understand—'

He had said he would not approach her with love while he was still her debtor, but now he knew that he had no choice. She had carried him over the barrier by the strength of her faith. He had nothing to do now but surrender.

To this fiercely self-sufficient man surrender was hard, all but impossible. But she could make it easy by turning it into a triumph.

He drew her to him again, exploring with hands and lips, and now she was free to yield to him utterly. Her fingers caressed the back of his neck, rejoicing in a freedom long desired and now achieved.

Gradually she could feel the tension drain out of him. She parted her lips invitingly, letting him in to explore her. The feel of his tongue against the inside of her mouth stimulated her to fever pitch and she seized him with a hand on each side of his head, falling back against the earth and drawing him with her.

The light robe slipped away easily, then her thin nightgown. Beneath it she was naked and, as though the sight inspired him, Rinaldo began to strip off his clothes. She helped him eagerly. This was no time for false modesty. She wanted him and she wasn't ashamed to let him know it. Her arms were wide open to receive him as he lay beside her, running his hands over her body.

'I've wanted to do this for so long,' he said hoarsely.

How could any man's touch be so gentle yet so demanding in the same moment? There was fire in every caress. She turned her body this way and that, letting him know silently what she wanted from him.

The earth beneath was full of the scent of ripeness. The springtime and the long ripening of summer was over. It was harvest now, for them as for the land.

He kissed her everywhere, meaning to inflame her passion until she was ready for him, but she was already there, impatient of delay. When he moved over her she parted her legs in willing acceptance. Then he was inside her, his weight pressing her into the soft earth.

Her love possessed her completely, driving out all else except the feeling that this man was hers to cherish, to fulfil, and even to protect. Protecting him must be done in secret, for it was something he would not understand. But her passion need be a secret no longer, and she claimed him totally, with a full heart that was all his.

Afterward they lay together, shaking, clasping each other as if for safety. It took time to come down from the heights. The view had been lovely, opening prospects that would last all their lives.

Rinaldo kissed her tenderly. 'Let's go inside,' he said softly. 'We have only begun.'

He took her hand, drawing her to her feet and helping her on with her clothes. Quietly they slipped through the trees and across to the house, where they climbed the stairs to her room, and closed the door.

Alex awoke to find herself tightly clasped in Rinaldo's arms. After keeping her at a wary distance he had finally abandoned his defences totally, drawing her in and making her a part of himself, as though he would never release her.

The night that had just passed was a fevered blur in her memory. They had possessed each other again and again, slaking a passion too long denied. After each loving they would sleep for a little and awaken with renewed desire. Their final sleep was one of exhaustion.

They awoke reluctantly, not wanting to let each other go.

'I suppose we have to get up,' he whispered.

'Yes, it's a new day.'

'A new day for us. I shall never let you go. You do know that, don't you. If you wanted to leave me, it's too late now.'

She smiled blissfully. 'That's all right then.'

He kissed her. 'It's not going to be easy. I love you, but it isn't going to turn me into sweetness and light.'

She gave a soft chuckle. 'Good. I wouldn't recognise you.'

'It's been so long since I loved,' he said in a low voice. 'I thought I'd forgotten how.'

'I'll always be there to remind you.'

Slowly they disentangled themselves and rose. Rinaldo pulled on his jeans.

'Before I leave,' he said, 'you'd better check the corridor, to see if the coast's clear. I don't want Gino to see me creeping out of your room.'

'No, he mustn't find out about us like that,' Alex agreed.

After a moment's hesitation he asked awkwardly, 'Will there be a problem about telling him?'

'No, there was never anything really between us. Just him flirting with me, at your command.'

'I didn't exactly—' he began uneasily.

Alex gave a burst of laughter. 'Oh, my love, my love! You should see your face! Be careful what you say. Gino told me everything.'

'Everything?' he asked, even more uneasily.

'Everything.'

His face was a delight. Alex could see that he wasn't used to bantering, and he was all at sea.

'Just what does "everything" include?' he asked cautiously.

'Well, if I say "two-headed coin" does that convey anything?'

He groaned and dropped his head in his hands.

'I'll kill him,' he muttered.

To Alex it was joyously funny, but she reminded herself that this was a man with too little experience of humour. In the years to come she would have to teach him to laugh and be happy. That would be her pleasure and her privilege. So she hopped beside him on the bed and put her arms about him, telling him without words that it wasn't the end of the world.

'Look—' he said desperately.

'Darling, it's all right. I think it's hilarious. That'll teach you to reject a lady before you've even met her. One part of me wants to say that you should simply have "taken your winnings". But the other part says it's better as it is. All that fighting we did—we needed it. We could never have got to know each other so well otherwise.'

'I could never have "taken my winnings",' he said. 'To approach you like that—' he shuddered. 'On the other hand I was angry enough for anything. Perhaps I—'

'Stop this.' She put her fingertips over his mouth. 'You don't have to explain yourself to me. I *know* you.'

'Yes, you do, don't you?' he said slowly. 'You've

known me all through right from the beginning. That night you said I was lonely, and like a fool I shut you out because you'd seen to the heart of me. I'd kept my heart locked away for so long that I couldn't take the risk of revealing it to you. So I rejected you, then I turned on you, accusing you of deviousness, to protect myself. And it was all useless, because there's no protection from love.'

'That's true,' she said, leaning her head against him. 'There's no protection for either of us, except each other.'

'Except each other,' he repeated. 'I was so alarmed by my own feelings that I left the house that night, running like a coward. When I heard you'd gone I thought it was safe to come home, but that just made everything worse. I couldn't bear the thought of never seeing you again. If you hadn't returned I'd have given in and come seeking you in England. The night you broke in and we struggled—do you remember?'

'Yes,' she said with a reminiscent smile. 'I remember everything.'

'Feeling you against me, beneath me—I swear you weren't safe. If Gino hadn't been there I'd have—well, I wanted to, anyway.'

'Mm! Me too.'

'But I didn't know what to say to you. You came back with flags flying, full of confidence. I knew you were free from that man, but I didn't know how you felt about it. So many times I've wanted to take you in my arms and say that nothing else mattered. But it did matter, so I started counting on the harvest. And I got it wrong because I could only hear my heart, not my head. I wanted to pay you, and then face you with pride.'

He saw her looking at him with gentle understanding,

and sighed. 'I got that wrong too, didn't I?' he said rue-fully.

'You think all the wrong things matter. Love matters. Not pride.'

'Is it really that simple, *amor mio*?'

'Yes, *amor mio*,' she said softly. 'It's really that simple.'

They kissed tenderly, but she could see that he was still troubled by one thought.

'Are you sure it will be that simple for Gino?' he asked. 'I thought once he was in love with you. Now I don't know.'

'He isn't. Oh, he made a big theatrical comedy of it, but I think that's just his way.'

Rinaldo nodded. 'You're right. All his life, everything had to be a production number.'

'But since I came back he's been a quieter, very polite, very respectful. Haven't you noticed?'

'Yes. And it's not like him.'

'He's probably just a bit embarrassed about backing off after all that theatrical ''passion'',' Alex mused. 'Especially after my engagement broke up.' She laughed suddenly. 'Oh, now I understand. Poor Gino. He was afraid I'd expect him to marry me, and he was trying to let me know, very kindly, that it's not on.'

Rinaldo's brow cleared.

'That would be it. But to be fair, he was probably madly in love with you at one time—for about two days.'

Alex raised an eyebrow at him. 'That's all you think I'm worth, eh?'

'No, but it's his record.'

They laughed together.

'Trust me, he'll be glad to have the problem solved,' she said.

She glanced into the corridor, saw that it was clear and signalled to Rinaldo. A brief kiss, and he was gone.

She followed him down a few minutes later and found him alone in the kitchen. Gino was just entering the house.

'Now?' Rinaldo asked her softly.

But Alex shook her head. 'No, I have something to tell you both first.'

He looked puzzled.

'Wait and see,' she said in a voice of teasing anticipation.

Gino came in, smiling when he saw Rinaldo.

'You look more cheerful than you did last night,' he said.

'And you're both going to look more cheerful when you've heard what I have to say,' Alex told them.

They looked at her expectantly.

'Enrico Varsi owes you money,' she said. 'Quite a lot of money if I've got my figures right.'

'But how?' Rinaldo asked.

Alex took a deep breath. 'Because he's been cheating you for years,' she announced.

'*What?*'

The exclamation was Gino's. Rinaldo was more wary.

'Alex, I really think that's very unlikely. Varsi is an eminent man—'

'Which makes it easier for him to get away with it.'

'He was also an old friend of our father, who trusted him completely.'

'Someone who trusts you is the easiest to deceive. I don't suppose it ever occurred to your father that his friend was stealing from him. It occurred to me as soon as I got a long look at your books.'

'I know you mean well,' Rinaldo said, 'And you're an

expert in British accounting practices, but this is Italy.
We have a different financial year, remember?'

'I know, and all sorts of other things are different.
That's why I've been taking a crash course in Italian
accountancy.'

'Where? How?'

'From a man called Tomaso Andansio. His offices are
just up the street from Varsi's.'

'Is that what I saw you looking at that day?'

'That's right. I knew I'd heard the name somewhere,
then I remembered we had some dealing with him in
London. Signor Andansio is brilliant and totally honest.

'I called him, and he let me spend a week in his office,
learning all I needed. When I showed him my evidence
he agreed there was a case, and gave me a whole lot of
reading to do. There's no doubt of it. Varsi's stolen a
fortune from you.'

She added wryly, 'But for that, your father might never
have needed a mortgage.'

Gino flung his arms about Alex in a fierce hug that
turned into an exuberant waltz about the room.

'You're a genius,' he yodelled. 'A genius, our good
angel, our glorious, shining star—'

'Yes, that's very nice,' Rinaldo interrupted him, 'and
I admit it opens interesting possibilities, but—'

'Interesting possibilities, you soulless man!' Gino protested, releasing Alex. 'Is that all you've got to say for
what Alex has done for us? You've never appreciated her
properly and I think it's time you—'

'I'm trying to be realistic,' Rinaldo cut him short
quickly.

'Rinaldo means he doesn't trust me to get it right,'
Alex said cheerfully. 'I anticipated that, so I'm arranging

for us all to go and see Signor Andansio. I dare say you'll believe him, seeing that he's a man.'

'Seeing that he's an Italian,' Rinaldo said, smiling at her and refusing to be provoked. 'I think visiting him is a very good idea, Alex.'

She went straight to the phone, followed by Gino who whispered in her ear, 'You're having a really civilising effect on Rinaldo. Keep up the good work.'

They drove into Florence later that day and in a few brief words the accountant confirmed everything Alex had said.

'It's a matter of how you define things,' he explained. 'Transfer certain things from one column to another and the whole picture changes. In between the two "pictures" there is a gap. A lot of money can fall into that gap, and an unscrupulous accountant can help himself. For years your tax liability has been less than the amount you paid, and since the cheques were routed through him—' He finished with an eloquent shrug.

'And Poppa never checked because he trusted him,' Gino sighed.

'It would have made no difference if he had checked,' Andansio said kindly. 'It's been very cleverly disguised, and you need to know what to look for. This lady—' he indicated Alex '—was particularly sharp-eyed to notice it in an unfamiliar environment. I've already told her that if she chooses to take the exams in this country there'll always be a position for her in my office.'

'I may just do that,' Alex said.

'I told you she was a genius,' Gino said.

'Can we get back to the point?' Rinaldo asked. 'We now know that Varsi has been robbing us all these years. What's the next step? The police? Can it be proved?'

'Oh, yes, but I think there may be another way of

dealing with him,' Andansio said. 'We show him our evidence and demand restitution, not only to yourselves but to all the other clients from whom he has undoubtedly been stealing. That will do them far more good than prosecution, and believe me, he can afford it. In return we'll have to promise to keep quiet.'

'Which leaves him free to prey on others,' Rinaldo pointed out.

'Oh, I don't think so,' Andansio said smoothly. 'I shall make it very clear to him that he's under my eye.'

'How much can he be forced to return to us?' Rinaldo asked.

Andansio named a sum. The three facing him stared in shock.

Gino gasped, 'But that's—'

'Almost as much as the mortgage,' Rinaldo murmured.

Alex said nothing. She merely smiled.

'I assume you will be wishing to move your affairs out of his hands,' Signor Andansio said.

'And into yours,' Rinaldo agreed.

'In that case, may I suggest that you leave matters to me? I believe I'll have good news for you quite soon.'

In a daze they went out into the light, and stood looking at each other for a few moments. Gino recovered first.

'A celebration!' he declared. 'Because we really have something to celebrate.'

It was almost evening. Gino grabbed both their hands and led them into the best restaurant he could find.

'Because we can afford it now,' he said. 'Waiter, what's the best champagne you have?'

He seemed carried away by exhilaration. It was as much as the others could do to calm him down, and then only for a short while.

Later that evening, after an excellent meal, they piled him into the back seat of the car, where he fell asleep with a smile on his face.

CHAPTER ELEVEN

THE whole area around Florence seemed to be one great harvest festival. Every night there was a party somewhere or other.

On the evening when the neighbours gathered at Belluna the air was brilliant with good cheer. Coloured lights hung from the trees, heavily laden trestle-tables were spread out in the open. All day Teresa, Celia and Franca had worked to lay on the best party in the district.

'You're beautiful,' Rinaldo told Alex as she emerged from her room in a floaty blue and white dress and white sandals. 'I want to tell everyone that you're mine. I wish we could do it tonight.'

'So do I, but we must tell Gino first, and I can't seem to catch him.'

Rinaldo nodded. 'Ever since Varsi agreed to repay the money, and we found that it covers our debt to you, he's been on a high. What is it?'

He spoke anxiously because a shadow had crossed Alex's face.

'What am I going to do with all that money?' she asked. 'I don't want cash, I want to be part of Belluna.'

'But as my wife, you will be a part of it.'

'I know, it's just that—'

But Rinaldo was growing in understanding.

'If that's not enough,' he said, 'you can pay for next year's fertiliser, and the repairs to the machinery, and the new barns. That will save us having to borrow from the bank as we normally have to. Then you'll have the financial stake that you want.'

'That's better,' she said.

'Don't look so cheerful. Do you know what fertiliser costs?'

'After all the accounts I've read? Of course I do. It's a wonderful idea.'

'And when we can pin Gino down we'll clear it with him,' Rinaldo said. 'After all, it's his farm too, and I shouldn't be making financial decisions without consulting him.'

'I'll bet he's not used to being consulted about anything,' Alex teased.

'You're making fun of me, aren't you?'

'Yes, and you'd better get used to it.'

'You must teach me. Now I suppose we should go downstairs and be ready for our guests. Where the devil is Gino?'

'These last few days he's always passing through, and I haven't even seen him today.'

'Yes, he told me he had some important business in Florence but he won't say what. It's been taking him to town on and off for days.'

'He must have a girlfriend,' Alex said triumphantly. 'And maybe he's going to bring her to the party tonight. Perhaps he's collecting her now, that's why he's late.'

The first cars were arriving as they went down and they were immediately engulfed in festivities. Within half an hour there were a hundred people, laughing, eating, sipping the best Chianti.

Alex looked around, feeling joyously at home at last. Just one more hurdle to go. If only Gino were here.

And then, suddenly, he was. They saw the lights of his car approaching, and the next moment he'd parked, leapt out and was being greeted with riotous enthusiasm by every guest. Gino was deservedly popular.

He went right round the party, kissing every woman there, even the oldest, leaving smiles behind him, until at last he presented himself to his brother and Alex.

'I'm sorry,' he said penitently.

'So you should be,' Rinaldo growled. 'This is Alex's first party here, and she's put a lot of work into it.'

'Alex will forgive me when she hears what I have to say,' Gino said, looking at her with a light in his eyes.

Seeing that light, Alex knew a sudden sense of alarm.

'Gino, dear, why don't you have a drink?'

'Let that wait. There's something I must say to you that's far more important. I've waited until now, but oh, *carissima* I can't wait any longer. I love you. I want to marry you.'

'Gino—'

'Hush, don't say anything. Let me show you this.'

He pulled a little box from his pocket and opened it. Inside glittered a ring that she could see was antique. It was exquisite, studded with diamonds and sapphires.

'I saw this in the shop window ages ago,' Gino said. 'And I thought then how I should like to give it to you on the day I asked you to be my wife. But when I went back for it they'd sold it to someone else, and it's taken me a long time to track him down and buy it. But it's mine now, which means it's yours.'

'Gino—' she whispered, devastated by what was happening, yet unable to stop it.

'Don't look so surprised, *carissima*. You've always known how I felt about you. Even when I was playing the fool, my heart was all yours. Or perhaps you didn't suspect how deep my love is. Maybe this will convince you.'

Before the whole party Gino went down on one knee, took Alex's hand in his and said, 'Alex, my love, will you please marry me? Will you be my wife?'

Alex felt as though she were moving through a nightmare. She should have silenced him but shock had held her transfixed.

In the silence, Gino took her hand and slipped the ring onto it.

Alex stared at the ring, her eyes full of tears as she thought how she must hurt him. How had she let this take her by surprise? she thought wretchedly.

But she knew the answer. Rinaldo had filled her thoughts to the exclusion of all else. Gino had existed only on the periphery.

Gino was still smiling up at her, not yet understanding her silence. Behind him she could see Rinaldo, his face pale and shocked. Imperceptibly she shook her head at him. What had to be done, she must do alone.

'Gino,' she said hesitantly. 'Please get up. Don't let's talk about this now.'

'What is there to talk about, darling?' he asked softly, rising to his feet and looking at her with eyes full of love.

'No,' she said, removing the ring and putting it back into his hand. 'Gino, I'm sorry—I can't—'

She saw the joy and certainty drain out of his face, leaving behind not disillusion but bafflement. He'd convinced himself of her feelings, and now couldn't believe otherwise.

Alex pulled herself together. 'Come with me,' she said, seizing his hand and drawing him away from the crowd.

Cheers followed them. Only a few heard had heard their exchange. The others saw them as lovers who wanted to be alone.

Gino thought so too, for as soon as they were through the trees he tried to take her into his arms.

'I'm sorry *carissima*, I shouldn't have done that in public.'

'Gino—'

'I know you'll forgive me when I tell you how much I love you. But surely you already know that?'

'No—no, I didn't. At first you seemed to be playing at flirtation, and since I came back from England you've stayed away from me.'

'I've hardly done that, but I've tried to show respect for your feelings. I knew how the breakup with your fiancé must have hurt you, and that you'd need time to get over him. I'm not an insensitive oaf, darling.'

'No, you're not,' she said. 'You're a sweet, kind boy—'

'I'm not a boy,' Gino said firmly. 'I may look like one sometimes next to Rinaldo, because I think he was born old. But I'm man enough to know that I love you with my whole heart and soul, enough to wait for you to be ready. Darling, must I wait longer? You know now how much I love you? Can't you love me now?'

'Oh, no,' she said softly, already in pain for him. 'Gino, I didn't understand, you always made such a joke of it.'

'Yes, I did in the beginning. I don't think I fully realised what my feelings were until you went away. It was unbearable without you, and I began to understand how deep it went with me. If you hadn't come back when you did, I would have followed you to England.'

She gave a gasp as she heard those words, so similar to the ones Rinaldo had spoken.

'I'd have followed you because I knew you were the one,' Gino said, 'the only one, different from every other woman I've fooled around with and loved for five minutes. It's not five minutes this time, but all my life and beyond—'

'No!' she cried, distraught. 'Don't say that. It mustn't be true. It can't be.'

A shadow crossed his face. 'Why can't it be true?'

'Because I'm not in love with you.'

He looked at her, almost as though the words conveyed no meaning to him.

'You're still in love with that man in England,' he said at last. 'I spoke too soon.'

'No, no, it's not him, it's—'

But she checked herself. This was no time to tell him about Rinaldo. Not here and now, in the middle of a party.

'Please don't say any more,' she begged. 'We'll talk about it later.'

'Yes,' he said. 'Later. I did it the wrong way, didn't I? I rushed you. I can wait.'

He gave her a brief smile and walked away back to the party.

She watched him, bitterly blaming herself for not seeing this coming. It was as Gino had said. He was no longer a boy but a man, with a sensitivity to her feelings that she had not suspected. It had misled her into thinking he didn't care.

As if to prove his new-found maturity Gino did not storm off alone, or sulk, but became the life and soul of the party. He danced every dance, flirted without end, and generally exerted himself to make things go with a swing.

The general opinion among the guests was that he must have attained his heart's desire, because he presented the picture of a supremely happy man. Only a few people noticed that he and Alex never went near each other for the rest of the evening.

At last the guests began to drift away. There were crowing goodbyes, songs yodelled up to the moon, and an air of happy satiety.

'Where's Gino?' Rinaldo asked Alex when they were alone.

'I last saw him half an hour ago. Oh, Rinaldo—'

'I know. It's terrible. He'll understand in the end, but he's bound to be sore after he declared himself so openly, in front of all those people.'

'He's been marvellous since then,' Alex observed. 'It must have been very difficult for him to be so bright and cheerful after what I said to him.'

'How much did you say?'

'Only that I didn't love him. It wasn't the right time to tell him the rest.'

She approached Teresa who was clearing away with the girls, and gave them some help. Later she found Rinaldo.

'Teresa says she saw Gino driving away,' she said.

'I guess he wants to think for a while. He'll feel better afterward.'

But despite his confident words he stood on the porch for half an hour, staring into the darkness.

'Don't let him come back and find you watching out for him,' Alex suggested gently. 'He's not a kid any more.'

'You're right. I can't get out of the habit of thinking of myself as a kind of second father. I'll have to now, won't I? But it's going to be hard, telling him.'

'Do you think perhaps—we shouldn't?' she asked unhappily.

But he shook his head.

'I can't give you up for any reason. Not just because I love you, but because you're necessary to me, as air and water are necessary. I love my brother, but even for him I can't do without you. Come inside with me now, for I need, very much, to be alone with you.'

In the darkness they climbed the stairs. Almost before they reached the top she was in his arms, kissing and being kissed with a determined purpose that thrilled her.

Rinaldo put out his hand and opened the first door he came to, which was his own room.

'I can't wait to get to yours,' he murmured, drawing her inside and shutting the door. He was already removing her clothes with urgent hands.

She helped him, stripping him even as he stripped her until they lay on the bed together and he took her into his arms for a long kiss that was part affirmation, part exploration. She loved this moment, when his tongue teased the inside of her mouth, rousing her gently and expertly to the pitch of desire that only he could create.

When he withdrew his mouth she could see that his face held the brooding expression that excited her so much. His great hand drifted over her breasts, enclosed one, caressing it with subtlety so that she was flooded with warmth.

For this above all she loved him, for revealing her own sensuality to her, showing her that the woman of desks and good order was only one facet, and not the truest one. The real Alex was a woman who lived for the primitive force that united them, and could relinquish herself totally to the man she loved.

For so harsh a man Rinaldo was an unexpectedly gentle and skilful lover. He waited for her to be ready, but he didn't have to wait long. She wanted him, wanted more of the shattering sensation that pervaded her, wanted everything.

When her moment came Alex drove back against him, urging him on with all her strength until they reached fulfilment together. She saw his face in that instant, and wondered at its mixture of awe and surrender.

He fell asleep first, and she propped herself up on her elbow, watching him with eyes that were passionately protective, but also curious. The chance to study him unaware did not come often.

His face was scarcely softer in sleep than in waking. The chin was still stubborn, the nose too strong for comfort. They would still fight. He'd warned her of that, and the starkness of his face told her that it was true. But that was all right. Fighting wouldn't suit everyone, but to them it would merely be an aspect of their love. And she could give as good as she got.

But she would be careful, because deep instinct warned her that he was more vulnerable than she, more easily hurt, less able to show it, and therefore more at risk.

His mouth intrigued her the most. It was not, at first glance, a sensual mouth; too firm, too wary, even in repose.

But she was no longer fooled by the look. She had kissed that mouth and felt it soften against hers. She had shared passion with that big, lanky body with its longs legs, powerful arms and skilful hands. No woman who had experienced that sensation could mistake his essential nature. He was a man who could love with every part of him, mind, soul and body.

After a long while she lay down, gazing into the darkness, looking back along the road that had brought her here.

Since coming to Italy she had discovered that the country had two faces. There was Italy of the smile and the song, of the rich colours, flowing wine and bright laughter. This was romantic Italy. This was Gino.

And there was another country whose past had been steeped in blood and vengeance, a dark, sombre place, full of sullen shadows, deadly feuds, anger, bitterness, danger. This was Rinaldo.

If a woman had once been delighted by the smile and the vibrant youth, why should she turn away from that to the other land, where a man with a face like granite and a soul to match offered only his darkness, and his need?

Why? Because she could not help herself. That was why.

She raised herself again and touched his face with her fingertips. Then she kissed him so softly that he did not awaken. He was hers, to have and to hold, to love and cherish. Because he needed her. And that was all there was to be said.

Rinaldo was in a mysterious place, one where he'd been before, but which had no name. He knew that he was waiting for something, but he did not know what.

His father was there again, looking at him with troubled eyes. But this was the moment when he always awoke, and the message was never delivered.

With a shudder he sat up in bed, his eyes open and staring. His whole body was shaking.

'What is it?' Alex said from beside him. 'Rinaldo, *wake up.*'

She shook him gently. At first she thought he was too far lost in his unquiet dream for her to reach him, but at last, to her relief, she felt him relax.

Still she could not be certain that he was awake, although his eyes were open. She touched his face gently.

'Rinaldo,' she whispered, 'talk to me.'

At last he seemed to focus on her. He looked drained, and when she put her arms about him he clung to her.

'Was it a bad dream?' she asked.

'No. Something came back to me at last. It's been there all this time, hovering just out of sight. I've tried so often to remember—'

'And now you have?'

'Yes. It was the day my father died. I got to the hospital before Gino and I had a few moments alone with him.

'When he saw me, he tried to say something. His face was swollen and he couldn't get the words out—just the words, "Sorry". He said that over and over. I can still see his eyes—they were desperate. He wanted so much to tell me something, but he couldn't manage it.

'I kept waiting for him to tell me, but then I realised that it wasn't possible. So I took his hand between mine and told him everything was going to be all right. He seemed quieter. And then he died.'

'What do you think he wanted to say?'

'I think it was the mortgage. He knew what was going to happen, and he was trying to tell me that he was sorry.'

Rinaldo shook his head as though trying to clear it.

'I don't know how I could have forgotten that,' he said. 'It was as though my mind just blanked it out.'

Alex took him in her arms, speaking gently.

'With all that happened that day, and the state you must have been in, it's not surprising. You needed to be ready to remember.'

'And I'm ready now, here in your arms. All this time— I blamed him—but he did try to warn me.'

'He never meant you to find out the way you did,' she said.

'That's right. He didn't just abandon us without a word, the way I felt he had. That might have been unreasonable, but it was how I felt. Now it's different. It's as though I'd got my father back again. You did that.'

Her heart sang at his praise, but she said, 'It would have happened anyway.'

'No, it happened because I found peace with you. That peace had to come first, before I could be reconciled with him. Now I am. He's in my heart once more, and I'll never lose him again—because of you.'

Suddenly he clung to her. 'Don't leave me,' he said desperately.

'Never in life. As long as you need me, I'll be here.'

'I'll always need you. There was no warmth or light before you came.' He rested his head against her. 'Suppose you'd never come here, and we'd never met?'

'But we did,' she murmured. 'Maybe we were always bound to meet. Do you remember that first day?'

'At Poppa's funeral? Yes.'

'I think I knew then that you were going to be something important in my life. I didn't know what, but I knew it wasn't going to be indifference.'

'No, we could never have been indifferent to each other,' he murmured.

'And in those days it looked like we'd be enemies.'

'Is that what we were?' he whispered.

'Oh, yes.' She smiled tenderly. 'We had to be enemies first before we could be anything else. It's not a bad way of getting acquainted.'

'Yes, we did that,' he agreed with a faint smile. 'Now we have to get to know each other in another way.'

'You think we don't know each other?' she asked softly.

He didn't answer at once, but he raised his head and their eyes held, full of deep, shared knowledge. They knew each other.

'I'm looking forward to the rest,' he said. 'Being with you every day, learning all about you, the things you like, dislike. Growing old with you, becoming part of you, making you part of me.'

'I *am* part of you,' she said. 'I always will be.'

'I feel as though I've spent the last years wandering in a desert. And you've brought me home.'

She kissed him repeatedly, not in passion but in tenderness. There had been passion and there would be passion again, but for now their embrace was an assertion of profound peace and trust between them. At last they slept again, still holding each other.

When Alex found herself drifting back to the surface she wasn't sure whether it was happening naturally or because of some other reason. Despite her feeling of fulfilment she was pervaded by an uneasy awareness of something wrong.

Slowly she opened her eyes.

Gino was standing at the end of the bed, staring at them both with a face full of shock and disillusion.

CHAPTER TWELVE

For a long moment Alex couldn't move. Inwardly she was weeping. Dear Gino, so generous and affectionate, the last man she would ever want to hurt! But his face was telling her that he was stricken to the heart.

Rinaldo was sleeping with his head against her, his whole attitude that of a man who had come home to the place where he belonged. Her arms were about him in a way that would have told Gino how things were between them, even if nothing else did.

'Gino!' Her lips formed his name without sound.

Still he neither moved nor spoke, while his face seemed to grow paler every moment. Alex reached out a hand to him.

Then he moved, backing away to the door, his eyes, filled with bitter betrayal, fixed on his brother and the woman he loved.

Despairingly she gave Rinaldo a little shake, awaking him. When he saw his brother he tensed and gave a soft groan.

Gino had reached the door, shaking his head as though trying to deny what his eyes saw. Then he vanished.

'Gino!' Rinaldo shouted.

He hurled himself out of bed, pulling on his jeans and racing to the door almost in one movement. Alex sat with her head in her hands, devastated by the sudden catastrophe, torn with anguish for Gino, who didn't deserve to be hurt like this.

'No,' she whispered. 'Please, no! Oh, Gino, Gino!'

Huddling on her clothes she went down to where Rinaldo had caught up with Gino in the room that led to the veranda. The tall windows had been thrown open, showing the low table, and the chairs where the three of them had spent happy evenings.

Gino was striding about the room, as though his pain was something he could leave behind. He turned when he heard Alex and she was shocked by his face.

It was as though all the youth had drained out of it, leaving it haggard and joyless. He looked from one to the other.

'Why didn't you tell me?' he asked. 'It wouldn't have been difficult, would it? Hell—the way you pulled the wool over my eyes, pretending to be enemies, letting me believe what I wanted. The only thing I don't understand is why?'

His eyes were cold and hard as he faced Alex. 'Did it give you some sort of pleasure to lead me by the nose?'

'I didn't—truly I didn't—'

'Don't insult my intelligence, Alex. All this time—'

'But it isn't all this time. You talk about Rinaldo and me pretending to be enemies, but it wasn't a pretence. When you've seen us quarrelling it's been real.'

'So what changed?'

'Nothing changed,' Rinaldo said quietly. 'What we felt for each other was there all the time, but we didn't know it. Or maybe we suspected, and were fighting it. I resented her at first, you know I did. I didn't want to fall in love with her, but I couldn't help myself because she's a wonderful—'

'*All right,*' Gino said harshly.

'I'm sorry,' Rinaldo said. He seemed cast down in a way Alex had never seen before, and she realised that in his own way he too was devastated. He loved his brother, and it was tearing him apart to quarrel with him.

'I'm sorry,' he repeated. 'I just hoped you'd understand—'

'I understand all I need to,' Gino said.

'Gino, listen,' Alex begged, 'Rinaldo hasn't taken anything that was yours. It was always going to be him. It took us both too long to realise it, but it's as he says. There was something there between us right from the start. All the time we were quarrelling, we were falling in love as well.'

As she spoke she'd moved forward so that she was standing directly before Gino.

'Please,' she said softly, 'please believe me, I'd do anything rather than hurt you.'

'Would you? You could have warned me.'

'But I didn't know how you felt. You treat love as a game, and you play it so well that that's all it seems.'

'It started that way,' he agreed, 'but then I found I was really in love with you.'

'I didn't know,' she said. 'If I had—I could have told you earlier that I could never love you.' He closed his eyes. 'Not as you want, anyway,' she said desperately.

He nodded. 'Not as I want,' he repeated softly.

'What happened at the party—I would have prevented that if I could.'

Gino made a despairing gesture. 'So I made a fool of myself in front of our neighbours. That's not important.'

He looked at Rinaldo. 'I came back here tonight to find you. I wanted to speak to you, ask your advice—there's a laugh. And I'll tell you another thing that's funny. The one thing I never thought of was that I'd find her in your bed.'

'I wish that had never happened,' Rinaldo said gravely.

'But Alex and I love each other, and we're going to be married. I didn't take her from you. The choice was hers.'

Alex hadn't thought it possible for Gino to grow paler, but suddenly his face seemed to become grey, the grey of death.

'Be damned to the pair of you,' he said with soft violence, and strode out.

'Gino—!' Alex cried, reaching for him.

'No,' Rinaldo stopped her following. 'He can't bear the sight of either of us right now. When he calms down he'll forgive us. But right now he needs to be alone, and we should respect that.'

Bleakly she nodded and let him lead her away. Together they climbed the stairs but at the top they paused, looking at each other. Then, as if by a signal, they went their separate ways. They couldn't be together again tonight, not in the face of Gino's anguished condemnation.

Alex went alone in her room and after a moment she heard Rinaldo's door close.

It seemed strange to come down in the early morning and not find Gino there. His handsome, smiling face, his clowning and his kind heart had always been part of her pleasure in Belluna.

She did love him. Not as she loved Rinaldo, with a dark, burning passion, but with the tender affection of a sister. But he wanted so much more from her that the chasm was unbridgeable.

She went out onto the veranda, hoping against hope that she would see him. But the morning was quiet.

Then her eyes fell on the chair where he always sat. The jacket he'd worn the night before was tossed down there. Alex ran her fingers over it, thinking of him putting it on before the party, slipping the ring into the pocket, planning how he would propose to her. He'd been full of young, eager love, sure of being loved in return. And it had turned to heartbreak.

There was a clatter as something fell to the floor. It was the ring he'd tried to give her. She sat down heavily and leaned her head on her hands.

After a moment she heard Rinaldo, felt his hand on her shoulder.

'That's how I feel too,' he said.

They sat together for a while, just taking comfort from each other's presence.

'Gino's gone away,' he said at last. 'His car isn't there, and some of his clothes are missing.'

'But he'll come back?' she said quickly.

'Of course he will. We just have to be patient. Everything will work out.'

Meeting his eyes, Alex saw that he didn't believe it any more than she.

'All these years,' he sighed, 'watching him grow up, being a second father to him, and now—dear God, what have I done to him?'

'What have *we* done to him?' Alex said.

'He's changed. Grown up. Last night it was like talking to an old man.' He sighed. 'Whatever happens now, we'll never see the Gino we knew.'

Alex forced herself to say the words that terrified her.

'How can I stay here if it's going to do this to him? If I go away—'

'No,' he said quickly. 'I can't live without you. I won't let you go.'

'I don't want to leave you,' she whispered, 'but—'

'No buts. We have the right to our love. Besides, your leaving wouldn't solve anything. Gino and I can't turn time back to before you came, and even if I could do that, I wouldn't.' His voice deepened, became tender. 'Never to have known you, loved you, to return to the half-life where you didn't exist—I couldn't do it.

'Thank heavens!' she said huskily. 'I was so afraid you'd want me to go.'

'Then you don't know me very well. I can't live without you now. The only reconciliation my brother and I can have is when he discovers the woman who will really be his love.'

He took her face between his hands.

'I told him we were to be married, although I hadn't asked you.'

'You know you didn't need to ask me. All I want is to stay here with you.'

'That's all I want too. Please God, we'll have many years together.'

They set the date of their wedding for three weeks ahead, and chose a small village church, on the edge of the farm. Many of the guests would be the farm-hands who, more than any others, had cause to rejoice at this marriage.

Wedding presents poured in, but the only gift they wanted was news of Gino, who had not returned.

He arrived unexpectedly one day while they were both out, and they reached home to find his car standing outside while he loaded luggage onto it.

His appearance shocked them. He had actually aged. His face, once so full of smiles, looked as though it would never smile again.

'I came for the rest of my things,' he said. 'But I waited for you. I couldn't leave without saying goodbye.'

'You're going for good?' Rinaldo asked. 'But this is your home.'

He did smile then, wanly and with irony.

'What do you suggest?' he asked. 'That we all three live together? You know we can't.'

They were silenced, knowing he was right.

'Where have you been?' Rinaldo demanded at last.

'I'm staying with friends while I sort myself out. I think I'll go abroad.'

'But you own part of this farm,' Rinaldo reminded him.

'I know. We'll have to make some kind of arrangement about that.'

'We've got time,' Rinaldo argued. 'At least stay here until the wedding—'

Gino stopped him. 'No,' he said with finality.

'But you will be there?' Alex implored.

'I don't know. Don't count on me.'

'There's something I've been wanting to tell you,' Rinaldo said heavily. 'I never thought it would be like this, but you must know. It's about Poppa. You've often asked me what happened at the hospital, when I was alone with him, and I could never tell you, because I couldn't remember. It was as though a curtain had been drawn across it, blotting it out from me. But that night— the night you came home—'

'Go on,' Gino said.

'It came back, while I was asleep. He spoke to me, and he tried to tell me about the money. He couldn't finish the words, but he tried. He didn't want to leave us to discover it the way we did.'

Gino nodded. 'Thank you,' he said at last. 'I'm glad you told me. It seems to give him back to us somehow.'

'Yes,' Rinaldo said at once. 'That's exactly what I felt.'

For a moment they were brothers again.

'I'd better go now,' Gino said. He hesitated before asking in a low voice, 'May I speak to Alex alone?'

'Of course,' she said at once.

Rinaldo nodded, and turned away to go into the house.

'It's all right,' Gino said. 'I'm not going to embarrass you. I just wanted to say—I don't know. I'd planned to say so much, and now it's all gone out of my head.'

'Forgive me,' she pleaded.

'There's nothing to forgive. You had the right to make your own choice. You'll never know how much I love you, because now I'm not free to tell you.'

'I think you just have told me,' she whispered.

He shook his head.

'That doesn't begin to say it. It was like a miracle to me to discover that such feeling could exist.'

'You'll feel it again, when you meet the right person for you.'

'Perhaps,' he said, and she knew he didn't believe her. 'But if that shouldn't happen—thank you.'

It was a moment before she could speak.

'You have nothing to thank me for,' she said at last.

'Oh, yes, I have everything to thank me for. And I do.'

She put out a hand to him but he flinched away, softening the gesture with a smile that it hurt her to see.

'The truth was staring me in the face all the time, wasn't it?' he said. 'That night when we had dinner, and I said you always brought the conversation back to Rinaldo. There was the clue, if only I had the wit to see it. It's nobody's fault but mine.'

'Come in and stay for a while,' she begged. 'Don't go like this.'

'I think I'd better leave.'

'At least come in and get your ring. You left it behind.'

'You fetch it for me. I'll wait here.'

She went into the house, turning in the doorway to see him standing beside the car, looking at her.

Upstairs she found Rinaldo and explained her errand. He followed her into her room and waited while she found the ring.

'When I give this to him,' she said, 'perhaps we—'

She was stopped by the sound of a car engine.

'Oh, no!' she gasped.

From the window they saw Gino's car vanishing in the distance.

She couldn't help herself then. She hid her face against Rinaldo and wept.

The wedding was both sad and happy. If things had been different Alex and Rinaldo would have bickered lovingly about which of them would claim Gino's services—she wanted him to give her away, and he wanted him as best man.

As it was, she was given away by Isidoro, her lawyer, and Rinaldo's best man was his foreman.

But all other thoughts faded as they stood together before the altar. This was her moment of glorious fulfilment, the moment that would inspire the rest of her life. Looking at Rinaldo she knew that it was the same with him.

Suddenly she heard a faint whisper in the church. Turning her head a little she managed to look over her shoulder enough to see the door.

A young man was standing there, silhouetted against the light. Alex couldn't see his face, but the sun just touched his hair, giving him almost a halo. He stood very still.

Then she thought she saw him move, coming forward to sit in a pew.

Of course he had come, she thought, happy and relieved. Whatever his pain, Gino's warm heart wouldn't let him stay away.

The priest was asking Rinaldo if he took her to be his wife. In a firm voice he declared his intention of doing so. Then it was her turn.

She forgot Gino. All her attention now was for the man she loved, making her his, as he was hers, for life.

But as the service ended and he kissed her, Alex murmured, 'Gino's here.'

'I know. I saw him by the door.'

It was all they needed to be happy. As they turned and walked back down the aisle together their eyes were searching row after row of faces, looking for the one face that mattered.

But he wasn't there. If he had ever been there, he had gone again.

The reception was held in the largest barn, hung with flowers and ribbons. The bride and groom laughed, drank toasts, and danced, but each was secretly longing for the moment when everyone would be gone, and they could begin their true life together. There was no sign of Gino.

When the last guest had gone they made their way across to the house, and there found an unexpected face.

'Bruno!' Rinaldo exclaimed with pleasure. 'We hoped to see you earlier.'

'I came with Gino, but he left at once and I felt I should stay with him.'

'I wish he'd talked to me,' Rinaldo said heavily. 'I've been trying to arrange things so that he'll have some money to live on, but he writes to say he won't take anything. He should accept something. Part of this place is his.'

'I know, but he feels he can't draw an income from the farm when he won't be here to do any work. With the money he won't accept you can hire more workers.'

Bruno's manner suddenly became uneasy and he couldn't meet Alex's eye. '*Signora*, he apologises for the way he ran away before. I believe his feelings overcame him that day. The only thing he wants—'

'Is the ring,' she said. 'I'll get it.'

Recently she had locked the valuable object in Rinaldo's office for safe keeping. It took only a moment to bring it out.

'Thank you,' Bruno said, slipping it into his pocket. 'And finally, there is this.' He proffered a letter. 'He wrote it after he left the church, and asked me to give it to you. And now, goodnight.'

He slipped away, leaving Alex staring at the letter in her hand. From the kitchen came the sound of Teresa calling the maids.

'Come,' Rinaldo said, taking her arm and drawing her towards the stairs. 'Let us read it where we can be certain of not being disturbed.'

The house was quiet as they closed the door of her bedroom behind them.

Standing by the window, still in her bridal gown, Alex took out the letter and read the words on the envelope. Her heart leapt as she saw,

To my brother and sister.

'Read it to me,' Rinaldo said quietly.

Alex opened the sheet within, and began to read.

I thought I couldn't bear to witness your wedding, but in the end I had to come, just for a few minutes. You looked so right together. Forgive me for not staying longer.

Forget my cruel words. I was half crazy and didn't know what I was saying.

I can't come back. We three cannot live under the same roof. But there's no hatred or anger.

Alex, I thought you were the woman for me, but you can't be, and I think perhaps Rinaldo needs you more. Take care of him. He needs to be cared for. But you already know that.

Perhaps, as you said, there's someone else, waiting for me to find her. Then she and I can share what the two of you share. I hope so.

God bless you both!

Your brother, Gino.

The letter ended with a typical Gino joke.

PS: You might name your first baby after me.
PPS: Only if it's a boy, of course.

'How like him to say that,' Alex said between tears and laughter.

'Yes,' Rinaldo said, and his voice too was husky.

He switched off the light. Outside the open window the countryside lay quiet under the moon.

'I wonder where he is now,' she said.

Instead of answering Rinaldo drew her away from the window.

'He is where he will find his own destiny,' he said, 'as

we have. Don't fear for him. He is a far stronger man than we thought, and his time will come.'

He drew her possessively into his arms.

'But now, *amor mio*, the time is ours. Let us waste it no longer.'

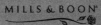